**It's a baby shower! You're invited...**

For Gwendolyn Tanner, soon-to-be mother
of twin baby girls—the subjects of
"Who's the daddy?" speculation.

Gwendolyn is registered at The Mercantile.

If you'd like to join the pool, we're taking bets on:

*Birth Date*
*Birth Weight*
*Paternity*

Call Sylvia Rutledge, owner of
The Crowning Glory Hair Salon, for more details.

Dear Reader,

What a spectacular lineup of love stories Harlequin American Romance has for you this month as we continue to celebrate our 20th anniversary. Start off with another wonderful title in Cathy Gillen Thacker's DEVERAUX LEGACY series, *Taking Over the Tycoon*. Sexy millionaire Connor Templeton is used to getting whatever—whomever—he wants! But has he finally met his match in one beguiling single mother?

Next, *Fortune's Twins* by Kara Lennox is the latest installment in the MILLIONAIRE, MONTANA continuity series. In this book, a night of passion leaves a "Main Street Millionaire" expecting twins—and has the whole town wondering "Who's the daddy?" After catching a bridal bouquet and opening an heirloom hope chest, a shy virgin dreams about asking her secret crush to father the baby she yearns for, in *Have Bouquet, Need Boyfriend*, part of Rita Herron's HARTWELL HOPE CHESTS series. And don't miss *Inherited: One Baby!* by Laura Marie Altom, in which a handsome bachelor must convince his ex-wife to remarry him in order to keep custody of the adorable orphaned baby left in his care.

Enjoy this month's offerings, and be sure to return each and every month to Harlequin American Romance!

Melissa Jeglinski
Associate Senior Editor
Harlequin American Romance

# FORTUNE'S TWINS
## Kara Lennox

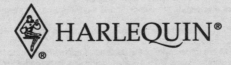

# HARLEQUIN®

TORONTO • NEW YORK • LONDON
AMSTERDAM • PARIS • SYDNEY • HAMBURG
STOCKHOLM • ATHENS • TOKYO • MILAN • MADRID
PRAGUE • WARSAW • BUDAPEST • AUCKLAND

Special thanks and acknowledgment are given to Kara Lennox for her contribution to the MILLIONAIRE, MONTANA series.

ISBN 0-373-16974-4

FORTUNE'S TWINS

# ABOUT THE AUTHOR

Texas native Kara Lennox has been an art director, typesetter, advertising copywriter, textbook editor and reporter. She's worked in a boutique, a health club and has conducted telephone surveys. She's been an antiques dealer and briefly ran a clipping service. But no work has made her happier than writing romance novels.

When Kara isn't writing, she indulges in an ever-changing array of weird hobbies, from rock climbing to crystal digging. But her mind is never far from her stories. Just about anything can send her running to her computer to jot down a new idea for some future novel.

## Books by Kara Lennox

### HARLEQUIN AMERICAN ROMANCE

840—VIRGIN PROMISE
856—TWIN EXPECTATIONS
871—TAME AN OLDER MAN
893—BABY BY THE BOOK
917—THE UNLAWFULLY WEDDED PRINCESS
934—VIXEN IN DISGUISE*
942—PLAIN JANE'S PLAN*
951—SASSY CINDERELLA*
974—FORTUNE'S TWINS

*How To Marry a Hardison

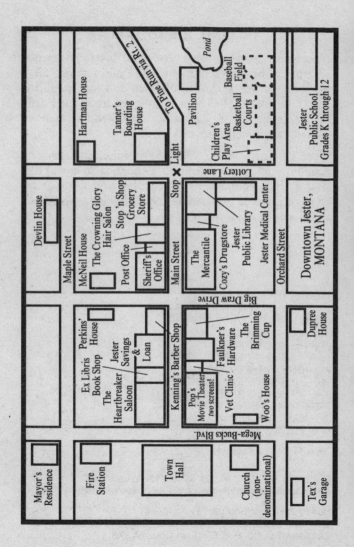

**Downtown Jester, MONTANA**

Mayor's Residence

Fire Station

Town Hall

Church (non-denominational)

Tex's Garage

The Heartbreaker Saloon

Ex Libris Book Shop

Jester Savings & Loan

Perkins' House

Kenning's Barber Shop

Pop's Movie Theater *two screens!*

Vet Clinic

Woo's House

Faulkner's Hardware

The Brimming Cup

Mega-Bucks Blvd.

Big Draw Drive

Devlin House

McNeil House

The Crowning Glory Hair Salon

Post Office

Sheriff's Office

Stop 'n Shop Grocery Store

Maple Street

Main Street

The Mercantile

Cozy's Drugstore

Jester Public Library

Jester Medical Center

Orchard Street

Dupree House

Stop

Lottery Lane

Hartman House

Tanner's Boarding House

To Pine Run via Rt. 2

Light

Pavilion

Pond

Children's Play Area

Basketball Courts

Baseball Field

Jester Public School Grades K through 12

# *Prologue*

"Oh, no, not again." Gwendolyn Tanner pulled her smoking casserole from her ancient oven, resisting the urge to let loose the worst curse she knew. This was the third dinner she'd burned this month, and it was all her oven's fault. The thing tended to malfunction when it got cold outside. Something about the thermostat. And since it was January in Jester, Montana…

Stella Montgomery, one of Gwen's permanent boarders at the Tanner Boardinghouse, trotted into the kitchen trailing a ball of yarn behind her, her current crochet project clutched in her hand, forgotten for the moment.

"I smell smoke," Stella announced, sounding worried. "Is something—oh, I see."

"This darn oven," Gwen grumbled as she tried to peel the burned top off her macaroni, cheese and sausage casserole. She was a good cook—an excellent cook. Cooking was probably the thing she did best. But this antique of a malfunctioning oven was going to ruin her reputation, and her boarders were going to starve to death. Unfortunately, she didn't have the money to replace the appliance. Not a lot of people stopped in Jester anymore. The economy in the small town had been in the tank for years. If not for Stella and the other two regulars, Irene Caldwell and Oggie Lewis, Gwen wouldn't be squeaking by at all.

Still, she didn't want to do anything else. Tanners had been running this house as a hotel or boardinghouse for more than a hundred years, and she didn't intend for that tradition to stop with her. Truly she loved her late grandmother's quaint Victorian house, with its turrets and cubbyholes and twisty staircases, though it was in dire need of repairs.

"I think we can salvage it," Stella said, diving into the casserole with a fork to pick out the burned bits.

"Some of it will be edible," Gwen agreed. "With a salad, and German chocolate cake for dessert, we should get by." She sighed and switched on the portable TV she kept in the kitchen. It was almost seven o'clock, time for the Big Draw. Gwen and several other people in Jester pooled their money and bought a bunch of tickets for the multistate lottery. They'd been doing it for eight years, but they'd never won more than a few dollars.

Still, Gwen did it more for the thrill than anything. It was fun to fantasize about what she would do if she won millions of dollars, or even a few hundred. A dollar a week wasn't much to pay for a fantasy.

"The jackpot's up to forty million," Stella said as she helped Gwen set the kitchen table. Usually they ate in the dining room, but since there would only be three of them tonight, there was no sense being formal. Irene was meeting with her book club, which was hosted by Regina Larson, the mayor's wife.

"Mmm, forty million," Gwen said dreamily. "Split twelve ways, but still. The first thing I'd do is buy a new stove."

"If I became an instant millionaire, I'd get the heck out of Jester," Stella said with a laugh, her tight blond curls vibrating. "We'll never find husbands here, honey."

"I don't want a husband," Gwen declared. "I'm happy with things just the way they are." She'd had to remind herself of that a lot lately. Oh, sure, she'd like a husband, children, a real family. But she didn't go out much, never went on a date. Heck, she'd grown up with most of the guys in Jester, and she had a hard time thinking of any of them in a romantic way. Some of them weren't all that bad-looking. Sheriff Luke McNeil was a hunk, and Dev Devlin, who owned the Heartbreaker Saloon, was pretty easy on the eyes. But even if Gwen was interested, she was shy and rather plain, so none of those guys gave her a second look.

"Oh, *pshaw*," Stella said. "I've had a man, and I've been alone, and let me tell you, having a man is better."

Stella, who was somewhere in her fifties, had never married, but she'd once been engaged. Her fiancé had died, and it was something she didn't talk about much. But sometimes Gwen sensed a deep sadness behind Stella's twinkly blue eyes.

Oggie Lewis, one of Gwen's other boarders, had a crush on Stella. Everyone but Stella knew it. Gwen was often tempted to mention it, but then she would hear her grandmother's voice: "Stay out of other people's business, and you'll never make enemies."

"Oh, here comes the draw," Gwen said, glad to have an excuse to change the subject. She turned up the volume on the TV.

The announcer drew out a Ping-Pong ball from the hopper. "Tonight's first number is…ten. Ten."

"Hey, that's one of your numbers," Stella said, checking the list Gwen kept on the fridge.

"The second number is…twelve. That's twelve."

"All right, another one!" Stella squealed.

Gwen felt an irrational bloom of excitement growing. One more number, and they could win five dollars. That was, what, forty cents apiece? That thought brought her back to earth.

"The third number is…twenty. Twenty."

"That's three!" Now Gwen really was getting a little excited. The first three numbers were matches. That had never happened before.

In what seemed like slow motion, the announcer called another number, then another. Each one was a match for Gwen's numbers. She reached out and grabbed Stella's hand. "This can't be real," she murmured.

Then the announcer reached into the hopper for the sixth and final number.

"Three," Gwen and Stella murmured together. "Three, three, three."

"The sixth and final number is…three."

Both women screamed. All six numbers were displayed on the screen for a few seconds. Gwen quickly compared them against her list, just to be sure.

She'd won the lottery. She and her friends.

Moments later, she heard screaming and whooping out in the street. Apparently she wasn't the only one who'd been watching the draw.

Gwen turned to Stella and hugged her. "I'm rich!"

"You're rich!" Stella agreed.

"What should I do now?"

"Let's go out in the street and celebrate! Sounds like everyone else is."

"Okay!"

As they ran through the house, grabbing coats and scarves, whooping and hollering like children, Oggie Lewis rushed downstairs to see what the commotion was about. Oggie, also in his fifties, was the vice principal at Jester High School. He was always dignified and nattily dressed. But when Stella shouted out the good news, he gave a little whoop of his own and ran out the front door without even a jacket—and it was snowing!

The Tanner Boardinghouse was on the corner of Main and Ashland Avenue. On Main Street, dozens of people were running around shouting, hugging each other, dancing, throwing things in the air. It seemed the whole town had gone crazy! But it was a nice crazy, Gwen mused giddily.

Jester had had little to celebrate in recent years. Some businesses, like the car repair shop around the corner from Gwen, had shut down, and others were hanging on by a spiderweb. Forty million dollars injected into the Jester economy would help not just the lottery winners themselves, but the whole town.

"Gwen, Gwen!" Gwen's best friend, Sylvia Rutledge, was running toward her, slipping and sliding on the snowy street. "We won!"

"I know," Gwen said, laughing as she hugged her friend.

"And it was your numbers. You're our lucky charm!"

"I know!"

Moments later, everybody was hugging Gwen. She was not used to so much attention, and she could feel her face heating from embarrassment and excitement.

"I can pay off my mortgage!" shouted Shelly Dupree, who owned The Brimming Cup, the only coffee shop in town. Gwen had heard that the petite brunette was in danger of losing her little café, left to her by her parents.

Only one person in the street wasn't celebrating. Wyla Thorne, who normally was one of the regulars in the lottery group, had decided not to buy a ticket last week. She'd said she was tired of throwing her money down a hole, and Jack Hartman, the town's veterinarian, had been recruited in her place. Now the pencil-thin redhead leaned against the old horse trough in front of the Heartbreaker Saloon, arms folded, a sour expression on her already pinched face.

"Oh, poor Wyla," said Stella, who was the only

person in town Wyla could truly claim as a friend. "What a terrible week for her to quit the lottery."

"I should say something to her," Gwen said. "But what?"

"Oh, leave her alone," said Sylvia. "She'll get over it, eventually. After we've all heard how unfair it is, about a million times."

Gwen was afraid Sylvia was right. Wyla did tend to feel sorry for herself a lot, though her last divorce had netted her a very profitable pig farm. She was about the only person in town who really didn't need the lottery proceeds.

"C'mon," Sylvia said, dragging Gwen by the arm. "We're gonna celebrate. It's not every day we become millionaires."

"Celebrate?" The idea was a bit foreign to Gwen. "How?"

"The Wild Mustang has Wet T-Shirt Night on Tuesdays."

"Oh, right." Gwen decided Sylvia's good fortune had caused a few screws to come loose in her head.

"I'm not suggesting we participate," Sylvia said. "But the place will be full of cowboys. And you *know* how I like cowboys."

Boy, did she. Sylvia was probably the most stylish person in Jester. She owned The Crowning Glory Hair Salon, and she was always attending hairstyling conventions in exotic places like Denver and Seattle, returning with the latest cuts—and the latest story of her exploits with the opposite sex. If she could hook up with a cowboy, that much better.

"Oh, come *on,*" Sylvia urged. "I'll drive."

"It's forty miles to Roan." Roan, North Dakota, was where The Wild Mustang was located.

"Exactly. If we go wild and make fools of ourselves, no one in Jester will ever hear about it."

Gwen was ashamed to admit she was tempted. She felt wild, free, actually light-headed from the shock of her sudden good fortune.

"You should go!" Stella urged her. "I'll make sure Oggie and Irene get fed. Honey, you hardly ever leave that house except to go to The Mercantile and the Stop 'n Shop. Once in a while, you're entitled to kick up your heels and have some fun!"

"You know, Stella, you're right."

Sylvia clapped her hands in childlike excitement. "Go put on your sexiest clothes and tease up your hair. We're going dancing!"

*Dancing!* Gwen thought as she threw on a pair of tight jeans and a red blouse with a ruffly, low-cut neckline. She was a millionaire, and tonight she was going to party, party, party.

Damn the consequences!

# Chapter One

Consequences.

Seven months after her lottery win, Gwen was certainly awash in the consequences of her wild night on the town. Her obstetrician had just given her the startling news. She wasn't just pregnant, she was carrying twins.

Dr. Sanders, an older, white-haired obstetrician who practiced in Pine Run, a larger town a few miles southwest of Jester, grinned broadly.

"Is something funny?" Gwen snapped. She wasn't normally a moody person, but her hormones were running amok these days.

"I'm sorry, Gwendolyn," he said. "It's just that, when you get caught, you really get caught."

Wasn't that the truth. She'd spent her life living by her grandmother's rules. Always sit up straight, eat your vegetables, wear clean underwear in case you're in an accident and never follow a man to his hotel room.

One little indiscretion—one!—and she was about to be a single mother with twins.

"I wouldn't smile at your expense," Dr. Sanders said, "except I know you're secretly delighted."

"In shock, more like it. I guess I should have known there was more than one baby in there." She patted her stomach, which was so swollen it made her look like she was near term, though she had two months of her pregnancy to go. Then she found her own smile. "But you're right. I was raised an only child, and I always wanted a brother or sister. My children will have each other." She paused. "But couldn't you have figured this out a couple of months ago when I bought all the stuff for the nursery?"

Dr. Sanders shrugged. "You wouldn't come in for a sonogram."

Again, he was right. She'd been trying to hide her unplanned pregnancy from her friends and neighbors for as long as possible—and that meant she couldn't make too many unexplained trips to Pine Run. But as she'd grown bigger and bigger, she'd realized she was being foolish. It wasn't as if she could hide the pregnancy forever. A couple of months ago, when she'd been delivering some baked goods to the Ex-Libris bookstore owned by her friend Amanda Bradley Devlin, Wyla Thorne had made some nasty comment about Gwen's weight, and Gwen had spilled the news.

The whole town had been shocked. She'd always been the good girl, the shy one, who followed the rules and never made waves. To suddenly become a single mother was like a tsunami.

As she drove back to Jester in her ice-blue Mercedes—one of her many indulgences since she'd received her lottery winnings—the news finally sank in.

Twins. Two children. What fun. But also, what a challenge for a single mother. Not for the first time, she wished she had a husband with whom to share the joys and fears of parenthood. But she could not find Garrett, the sexy hunk she'd met at The Wild Mustang that cold January night. She'd left him her phone number, but he hadn't called. And she didn't know his last name or where he lived.

As she drove the familiar Route 2 toward Jester, she couldn't stop her thoughts from migrating back to that wonderful, magical night when she and the other Main Street Millionaires—that was what the press had dubbed them—had won the lottery. She'd been riding high, floating in a surreal cloud of joy and optimism. She and Sylvia mentally spent their winnings a hundred times over on that snowy drive to Roan, North Dakota, though Gwen had put most of her money in blue-chip stocks and bonds for the future.

When they'd arrived at The Mustang, the place was rocking. As Sylvia had predicted, drunk cowboys were in abundance, and the moment they walked through the door, they had more drink offers and dance invitations than they could handle.

Gwen wasn't that big on cowboys, drunk or otherwise. Her father, whom she'd never met, had tricked her mother into marriage by pretending to be a prosperous Montana rancher. Her mother didn't find out the truth until too late. Willie Tanner was a con man and worse, and his "ranch" was a broken-down pig farm, heavily in debt. After eloping with Gwen's mother, who'd been a minor heiress from Billings, he'd wasted no time cleaning out her bank accounts to pay off some rather nasty creditors—the kind who favored cement overcoats—then disappeared, leaving Gwen's mother destitute, stranded, estranged from her family, and pregnant. She'd died shortly after Gwen's birth.

Gwen's paternal grandmother, Abigail Tanner, had taken in Gwen as an infant. Though she'd long ago turned her back on her no-account son, she'd willingly, lovingly, raised his daughter. One thing Grandmother had drilled into Gwen's head was not to let any smooth-talking men talk her out of her better judgment—or her bloomers.

"What did I tell you?" Sylvia asked as she sat down to sip her beer, taking a break from the dance floor. "Wall-to-wall cowboys. Are you having fun?"

"Yeah, actually, I am." She'd received more attention from men that night than she had in her whole life. It might have been the sexy clothes or the dark red lipstick. Or it might have been her attitude. For once in her life she felt strong, confident, powerful. She could do anything!

"You haven't been dancing," Sylvia pointed out.

"Dancing's not really my thing. But I love watching. And I've got enough free booze to last a month." Several eager bucks had sent drinks to Gwen's table, but she was still nursing the same Shirley Temple she'd started with. She'd volunteered to be the evening's designated driver.

Sylvia sighed. "What am I going to do with you? Listen, I've found a live one, and we want to get out of here. I'll give you my keys, and you can drive my car home. I'll get a room at the hotel later and find my way home in the morning."

Gwen gasped. "You're leaving with a complete stranger?"

"We aren't strangers anymore." Sylvia winked.

Far be it from Gwen to rain on Sylvia's parade. "All right. But please, be careful."

"I will. And you—try not being so careful for a change, huh? If you can't find a guy in this smorgasbord, you're doomed to a life of spinsterhood."

That word echoed in Gwen's mind for a long time. She wasn't a spinster. That was a stupid word, anyway. She chose to be single.

Didn't she?

Just then, she spotted a very good-looking man a few tables away. He wasn't a cowboy, either. In fact, he might as well have been wearing a sign that said, "city boy." His black hair was short, expertly cut. In his khaki slacks and tailored shirt, he looked more like a businessman of some sort. And, like her, he was on the sidelines, watching the action rather than participating. He appeared to be alone, too.

"Spinster," Gwen muttered. "I'll show her spinster." With a determined toss of her head, she stood, picked up the watery Shirley Temple, and strode to his table.

He glanced over at her as she approached, and she could see that his eyes were blue, a deep, intense hue that seemed to see straight to her core. Her heart jumped unexpectedly.

*No turning back now.* "Hello. Mind if I sit here?" Her voice sounded like it could have been someone else's. Where had that B-movie dialogue come from?

He stood and pulled out the chair next to him. "Please."

She sat down, acutely aware of the man just a few inches from her now. She could feel his body heat, smell a faint whiff of his aftershave.

"I've been watching you," he said. "You're not comfortable here, are you?"

"It was my friend Sylvia's idea. We're celebrating."

"Celebrating what?"

"A windfall." She didn't elaborate. People with money made easy targets. Her mother's experience had taught her that. "This isn't your favorite place, either."

"I was just about to leave."

"Oh."

"But now I won't. Want to dance?"

Adrenaline shot through her. This gorgeous guy was actually responding to her flirtation! "I'd love to."

Gwen was a terrible dancer, so she was relieved when a slow country song came on as she and her new acquaintance hit the dance floor. Slow dancing didn't require much skill. She just had to put her arms around the guy and rock slowly back and forth.

His muscles were hard beneath his crisp shirt, and he smelled of soap and starch and that alluring scent of expensive aftershave. Gwen was half in love with him before the song ended.

They kissed after the second slow dance. He tasted faintly of scotch, she remembered. Then he took her to his hotel. He had a suite at the Ramada, one of only two hotels in Roan.

Gwen had never behaved like this, but this night, it felt perfectly natural. They shared few words. Talking didn't seem to be necessary. She'd connected with Garrett—that was his name—on some elemental level. She wasn't at all embarrassed when he took her clothes off. Though she was slender, she'd always thought her breasts were too small. But the way Garrett kissed and caressed them, he made her feel they were the most perfect breasts in the world.

All of her felt perfect. She wasn't a sophisticated lover, but with Garrett she'd felt skillful, confident, sexy. Everything she did was right. Everything *he* did was perfect.

Gwen wasn't a virgin. She'd had a brief, secret relationship with a man staying at the boardinghouse one summer when she was nineteen. It was shortly after her grandmother had died, and she'd been struggling with the boardinghouse and desperate for an intimate connection. Instead the experience had turned out painful and awkward. Sex with Garrett, on the other hand, was like dancing a perfect ballet. And for the first time in her life, a man's caresses had brought her to the pinnacle of pleasure.

They'd slept curled in each other's arms. In the morning, he'd scrubbed her back in the shower and combed the tangles out of her hair with painstaking gentleness. Then he'd fed her a sumptuous room-service breakfast. But with daylight came harsh reality. She had to get home. Sylvia would want her car back, her boarders would want breakfast. Worst of all, there would be embarrassing questions to answer if she didn't get home soon.

She'd used Garrett's elegant fountain pen to scribble her name and phone number on a piece of hotel stationery. Then, with one final, searing kiss goodbye, she'd left him.

He hadn't called. He'd *promised*. Then he'd forgotten her.

She'd cried on Sylvia's shoulders for days. Then she'd found out she was pregnant, and she'd cried for another week. She'd tried to locate Garrett to tell him of his impending fatherhood. But all she had was a first name. He'd told her little about himself, so she had nothing to go on.

Gradually she'd pulled herself together and started planning her future. At least she had plenty of money to raise her child—children, she corrected herself. Two girls, according to the sonogram. She'd furnished the nursery with a fanatical eye for detail, started a trust fund for a college education, drawn up her will. She'd thought of everything.

Except the possibility of twins.

She wanted to share the news with Sylvia, the only person who knew the true circumstances of how she'd gotten pregnant. But Sylvia was in Billings, arranging for the delivery of some fancy new sinks—purple ones—for her salon. Gwen decided she would stop in The Brimming Cup and have some herbal tea. Shelly, who had recently married Dr. Connor O'Rourke, was pregnant, too, and the two mothers-to-be liked to compare notes.

As she made this decision, a vintage Jaguar passed on her left. Wow, nice car. Maybe she should have gotten one of those, instead of the more practical Mercedes.

She glanced down at her speedometer and realized she was only driving forty-five. No wonder the guy had passed her. All that reminiscing had distracted her from her driving. Vowing to be more alert, she pressed on the gas.

JESTER, MONTANA. Eli Garrett had never thought to look for Gwen here. And he'd definitely been looking. Though he was no monk, he'd never had a passionate night like the one he'd shared with delicate, auburn-haired Gwen. In that bar full of cheap perfume and teased hair, she'd seemed so fresh, like a daisy among overblown roses. The fact she couldn't dance had endeared her to him. Her natural shyness, which she attempted to overcome, was the most charming quality he'd ever seen in a woman. He'd become almost obsessed with her. Any time his car restoration business took him to towns within a hundred miles of

North Dakota, he asked around about her. But the woman had vanished like a wisp of smoke.

It would have been much simpler if he'd simply called the number she'd left for him. Unfortunately, he'd managed to spill his room-service coffee all over the sheet of stationery she'd written on. The blue ink had run in a hundred different directions, and no amount of blotting or cursing would bring it back. He'd even hired a documents expert to examine the paper—that was how desperate he was. But no luck.

Just when he'd begun to resign himself to the fact that the most intriguing woman he'd ever met was out of his reach forever, a stroke of luck had brought her to his attention. He'd been picking up a 1928 Nash Coupe some rancher had found in a barn, covered with hay, just outside of Denver where Eli lived. The rancher's wife had insisted Eli come inside for some lemonade, since it was ninety degrees outside, almost unheard of high in the Rockies, even in mid-August. There, on her kitchen counter, a photo on the front page of a newspaper had jumped out at him.

It was Gwen. No doubt about it. Her face had invaded his dreams so many nights it was etched into his brain.

''Main Street Millionaires have a new reason to celebrate,'' the photo caption read. The photo depicted an attractive couple, identified as Sam and Ruby Cade, who had apparently thrown a party when they'd reconciled their marriage. Gwen was off to the side of the photo, holding a huge cake.

And she was pregnant.

For a few moments, all Eli could do was stare. Was she married, then? Or…mentally he counted back the months. Was it possible the child was his?

"Can you believe that?" the rancher's wife said when she noticed Eli's interest in the photo. "Every time one of those Main Street Millionaires moves a muscle, somebody has to plaster the news on the front page. I mean, who cares?"

Apparently a lot of people did. When a small, hard-scrabble town in Montana suddenly had more millionaires per capita than any town in the U.S., it was news, and the lottery win in Jester had captured the fancy of the whole country. Though Eli hadn't followed the story, he'd still heard about it.

Now he wished he'd paid more attention. His search for Gwen could have been shortened considerably. No wonder she'd been celebrating the night they'd met.

"My cousin sent me that paper," the rancher's wife said. "It's a few weeks old. He—my cousin, that is—invested in some hotel development scheme in Jester. Seems the mayor there is trying to turn the town into a tourist attraction. But they can't find any land to build the hotel on, so the whole deal's probably awash."

Eli was hardly listening. He gulped down his lemonade, said his goodbyes, and jumped into his tow truck. Once he had the Nash safely tucked into one of his garage bays, he climbed into his silver 1960 Jaguar and headed for Jester, Montana. His GPS gave him the driving instructions.

Now that he was in Jester, he didn't know quite where to start. It was certainly a quaint town. A bit rundown, but here and there were signs of economic recovery. A shiny new Cadillac was parked in front of a general store, called simply The Mercantile. The hardware store was getting a face-lift. And a bronze statue of a bucking horse, in front of the Jester Town Hall, gleamed with a recent polishing.

In a town this size, all he needed to do was ask anyone about Gwen, and someone would enlighten him. Where to ask—the barbershop? Several older men sat outside Kenning's Barbershop, shooting the breeze.

Then Eli saw an inviting coffee shop, The Brimming Cup. Perfect. He hadn't had lunch. And now that he was so close to finding Gwen, he was curiously hesitant. What would he do if she was married? Or what if he was about to become a father? He hadn't thought through what he would say.

Or how he would feel.

A bell above the door announced Eli's entrance into the large, airy diner. The place had a '50s feel to it, with a long Formica, chrome-trimmed counter and stools topped with light blue vinyl. An old Wurlitzer jukebox in the corner appeared to be operational, though currently it was silent.

A pretty young woman with sleek, chin-length brown hair smiled at him from behind the counter. "Sit anywhere you like. You just missed the lunch rush, so the place is all yours."

He was, indeed, the only customer. He chose one

of the four booths that faced the front windows and perused a laminated menu that had been stuck behind the salt-and-pepper shakers.

As the waitress emerged from behind the counter, Eli could see that she was pregnant. Jeez, was it something in the Jester water supply? She set a glass of water, a napkin and some silverware on the table.

"Know what you want?"

"A hamburger, please, lettuce and tomato only. And a cup of decaf." Normally he liked his caffeine, but he was already wired.

The waitress scribbled on her pad. "Be right up."

He'd just taken his first sip of the coffee, which was surprisingly good, when the bell over the door rang. Eli looked up, curious to see who might be joining him, when he almost choked on his coffee.

It was Gwen! If this wasn't fate stepping in, he didn't know what was.

"Hi, Shelly," she said with what could only be described as a weary smile. "I could sure use a lemonade and a slice of lemon meringue pie." She sat at a table a short distance from him, but she didn't seem to notice him there, which gave him the opportunity to study her more thoroughly.

She was still pregnant—even bigger than she'd been in the newspaper photo. But rather than detracting from her beauty, her swollen belly made her even prettier. She looked earthier, more womanly, less fragile than he remembered. Though it was a cliché, he couldn't help thinking that she glowed.

She wore a simple, peach-colored maternity dress

and leather sandals, and her magnificent hair was pulled back in a bun. Nothing about her screamed "millionaire."

No jewelry—not even a wedding ring, he noted with interest. But he knew that sometimes women's hands swelled when they were pregnant, so the absence of a ring didn't mean anything.

He should go over to her table, talk to her. But suddenly he was scared. He didn't want to find out she was married, or involved with some other man. But then, was the alternative any more palatable? Was he ready to discover the child she carried was his?

The waitress, whom Gwen had called Shelly, reappeared with a cold drink and a slice of pie for Gwen. "I wish I could eat like you do," Shelley said wistfully. "I just found out I'm borderline diabetic, so no sugar."

Gwen looked concerned. "Shelly, are you okay?"

"It's not a big deal. Lots of women become diabetic during pregnancy. It just means I have to be careful. But one thing I was looking forward to was eating for two—with no penalty."

"No penalty? I'm as big as a horse."

"You'll lose it all once you have the baby."

Gwen glanced nervously in Eli's direction. He quickly hid behind the menu, wanting to eavesdrop some more. He'd never thought women discussing their pregnancies was particularly interesting—until now.

Peeking over the menu, Eli watched as Gwen motioned for Shelly to sit down. The two women had a whispered conversation. Shelly gasped at whatever Gwen told her, then grinned with delight.

"That is so cool! Wait 'til everyone hears!"

"Don't tell anyone yet, huh, Shelly? You know it'll get to the media, and I'm so sick of reporters. Frankly, I can't imagine why the press is still interested in the Main Street Millionaires."

"At least they're not staying at your boardinghouse anymore."

"Thank goodness. That Harvey Brinkman from the *Plain Talker* was a real pig."

"I sure wish I knew who it is that's leaking private information to the press," Shelly said. "I'd wring their neck."

Eli decided he'd skulked behind his menu long enough. He still didn't know what he would say to Gwen. He supposed he would just wing it.

"Order up!" a gruff voice called from the kitchen. Shelly hopped up to get it. At the same time, Eli stood and walked determinedly across the diner to Gwen's table. "Mind if I sit here?" he asked, using the same exact line she'd used on him at The Wild Mustang.

Gwen looked up and promptly choked on her lemonade. "Garrett!"

"Eli," he corrected her. "Eli Garrett. Are you okay?"

She gave one final cough. "Yes, I'm fine."

"Can I sit down?"

Gwen cast a worried glance toward Shelly, who was fast approaching with Eli's burger, a questioning look on her face.

"Yes, sit." Her face looked alarmingly pale. "Shelly, this is a...an old friend of mine, Eli Garrett. Eli, this is Shelly O'Rourke. She owns The Brimming Cup."

Eli murmured a pleasantry, as did Shelly, who set his hamburger on Gwen's table. "Shall I bring over your coffee?" she asked Eli.

Gwen looked uncomfortable with the situation, but Eli wasn't about to back off. He had to talk to her. "Yes," he answered Shelly. "Please."

As soon as Shelly had brought his coffee mug and left them alone, Gwen wasted no time starting the conversation. "You pick a fine time to show up. Seven months and not a word."

"I'm sorry about that. I tried to find you."

"How hard could it have been? I left my phone number."

"I spilled coffee on it. The ink ran everywhere, and when I was done cleaning up the mess, there was no sign of your number. I asked everybody in Roan if they knew you. You'd said something about a boardinghouse, so I looked up every boardinghouse in North Dakota trying to find you."

"So is this just a happy coincidence?"

"Sort of. I saw your picture in a newspaper."

"Ah. I see." If her spring-green eyes had looked wary before, now they appeared downright hostile. Apparently she didn't believe him.

"I wanted to see you again," he said. "Honestly. You'll never know how much. We had the start of something good and—" He took a sip of coffee and forged ahead. "Look, before I go on and make a jerk of myself, I just have to ask you one thing. Are you married?"

"No." She avoided his gaze.

"Then…is it mine?"

Gwen looked around worriedly and lowered her voice to a whisper. "We do need to talk, but not here. Can you meet me at the Tanner Boardinghouse in a few minutes? We can have some privacy there."

He took that as an affirmative answer to his question. His stomach swooped. He was going to be a father. He felt strangely elated at the news.

Ironic, given his origins.

"The boardinghouse is on the corner of Main and Ashland—or, rather, Main and Lottery Lane. Mayor Larson has changed some of our street names."

"I'll see you there, then."

She started to get up, but he stopped her. "Gwen?"

"Yes?"

"You look really fantastic. That dress is a very nice color on you."

"Oh. Thank you." Again, she wouldn't meet his eyes. This time she made good her escape, not even paying for her pie and lemonade.

Eli took a bite of his hamburger, but found he had no more appetite for it. He took his check to the register, where Shelly rang him up. "I'll pay for Gwen's bill, too," he said. "She seems to have forgotten."

Shelly's expression was distinctly unfriendly. "Don't worry about it. Gwen can eat here on the house any time she wants. Folks in Jester look after each other.''

Her message was clear. He'd better not do anything to hurt Gwen. But maybe it was too late for that. He'd gotten her pregnant, then abandoned her. How much more hurtful could it get?

# Chapter Two

Though it was only a couple of blocks between The Brimming Cup and the boardinghouse, Gwen drove her car. She didn't walk anywhere these days, except for the mandatory thirty minutes she walked every morning when it was still cool, ordered by her doctor. Now it was pushing ninety degrees, and Gwen felt limp as the faded Montana flag that hung in front of the Jester town hall.

Why, of all times, did Eli have to show up now? Just when she'd gotten used to the idea she would never see him again, he waltzes back into her life, twice as sexy as she remembered.

And she was bucking for a prize for best imitation of a water buffalo.

She might have been prepared to believe his story about the smeared ink and his frantic, months-long search for her. Down deep she was a romantic, and he wouldn't have had difficulty convincing her he was smitten. But then he'd revealed how he'd found her. He'd seen her picture in the paper, which meant he knew she was worth over a million dollars.

He'd capped it all off by telling her she looked good. If she'd been skeptical at first, that comment had sealed Eli Garrett's fate. There was only one adjective to describe her—huge. *Fantastic* was way out of the ballpark.

She pulled her Mercedes into the carriage house. She still wasn't up to facing Eli. She wished she could have told him to go away and come back next week, when she would be better prepared. But her grandmother hadn't raised her to be rude. He'd come all this way, and she supposed she owed it to him to find out what he wanted.

*You know what he wants,* her grandmother's voice rang inside her head. *A million dollars can make any woman beautiful.*

She climbed the front porch steps of her frilly Victorian house, glad she'd asked Eli to meet her here on her home turf. She was queen here at the Tanner Boardinghouse. She felt her strongest here, where her grandmother's memory was a constant, comforting presence.

She started to open the front door, then hesitated. At least a breeze was blowing across the front porch. Inside it would be stuffy. She'd already hired a company from Pine Run to put central air into her house, but they were backed up and hadn't yet started the job.

She decided she would meet Eli here on the porch. Relieved not to have to walk one step farther, she sank into a delicate white-wicker rocker and waited for Eli, rehearsing what she would say to him.

She would be firm, businesslike and unemotional, she coached herself. She would be appreciative of his interest in her, but insist that he need not trouble himself. She had gotten on with her life, she would say, and he probably should get on with his and not give her another thought.

No doubt he'd figured out that the offspring in her belly was his. She hadn't denied it. But once she made it clear she wouldn't be easy pickings—and neither would her bank account—he probably wouldn't be thrilled by his impending fatherhood.

She intended to give him an easy out.

Less than five minutes after she'd sat down, she spotted Eli walking toward her down Main Street, and her mouth went dry. Even from a distance, he was just about the most handsome man Gwen had seen. He had a loose-limbed walk, not brisk but not ambling, either. Like he had somewhere to go but he was going to enjoy getting there.

He smiled at the guys in front of the barbershop, then stopped to pet Buck, the stray shepherd mix Jack Hartman and his wife, Melinda, had adopted. Buck had his head stuck out the window of Melinda's green-and-white Dually, which was parked outside the hardware store.

Everyone stared at Eli without trying to look like they were staring. Before the lottery win, few strangers crossed Jester's town limits. Now all kinds of people came to get a look at the so-called richest town in America, and not all of them were harmless. A few months ago, Amanda had been accosted by a drunk drifter outside The Heartbreaker Saloon.

Eli crossed the street and mounted the steps to Gwen's house.

Gwen gave him a little wave. "I hope you don't mind if I don't get up."

"Please, don't." He sat gingerly on another wicker chair. His imposing height and muscular body challenged the delicate piece of furniture, but it held him. He took in Gwen's view of the park.

"Nice town you have here."

"It's special," she agreed. "I've lived here all my life. Even in hard times, when the boardinghouse was barely squeaking by, I never considered leaving."

"I've never lived outside of Denver. I always thought I'd be bored in a small town."

"Probably not this one," she said. "Not lately, anyway."

"I guess the lottery has brought some pretty big changes."

"You could say that." In fact, it was an understatement. "The whole town has gone crazy. First, we were inundated with nosy reporters. Then our mayor, Bobby Larson, tried to turn Jester into a tourist attraction. He wants to build a hotel on the park property. Can you imagine?"

"I heard something about that—just this morning. One of my customers knows someone who actually invested in the hotel."

Gwen gasped. "How can Bobby solicit investors for a hotel that doesn't exist?"

Eli shrugged. "Sounds like your mayor is involved in some shady dealings."

Gwen sighed. "If Bobby manages to push this project through, it'll ruin my view. Then there's the noise, the traffic—shoot, maybe I should sell after all."

Eli looked horrified. "Sell this beautiful old house?"

She shook her head. "No, I wouldn't really do that. But someone's been trying to buy it from me. Over the past few months I've received several anonymous offers, each higher than the last."

"This is a great house," Eli said, looking around. "You've restored it beautifully."

"You should have seen it last year. It looked more like that one next door." She nodded toward her neighbor's house. Another enormous Victorian, it was all but falling down. Her neighbor, an elderly widow, had moved out a couple of years ago to live with her children in Florida. The house had been on the market, but no one had bought it, and it continued to deteriorate. "But I guess you didn't come all the way to Jester so we could talk about house restoration."

"No." He cleared his throat. "Gwen, the baby is mine, isn't it?"

"Well…" She swallowed, her throat suddenly thick. "Okay, Eli, I'll give it to you straight. I don't know who the father is. I had a rather…wild winter. I guess I went crazy along with everybody else."

"I see." He didn't look particularly relieved over her lie. "You could find out the father's identity.

DNA testing has become fairly routine for that sort of thing.''

''I'm not the messy-paternity-suit type. Anyway, what end would that serve? Make some guy feel guilty and resentful, give him a responsibility he doesn't want? I don't want any child of mine to have to deal with a less-than-committed father.''

''I see,'' Eli said again. His words were soft, but his nostrils flared.

Gwen didn't understand this at all. She was giving him an out, an escape hatch. Didn't he realize that?

''I didn't mean to get pregnant,'' Gwen said, ''but now that I am, I'm very happy about it. I have plenty of money to raise a child alone, so that's not an issue. I'm prepared to move on with my life, and I certainly don't want to tie myself and my offspring to some guy I met in a bar. Or wherever,'' she added quickly.

''I see.''

''Stop saying that. I get the feeling you don't see at all. Why should a man have to pay the rest of his life for one passion-induced moment of insanity in a hotel room—or wherever?''

''Why should a woman?'' he countered.

''But I want a baby,'' she said.

''Maybe the guy wants a baby, too. You won't know 'til you ask him.''

''How can I ask him if I don't know who he is?''

''You can find out.''

''We're talking in circles.''

Eli stood and walked over to the railing. ''How many…candidates are we talking about?''

"Oh, I don't know," she said breezily. "I wasn't keeping count."

He watched her through narrowed eyes. Well, great. Now Eli thought she was a slut.

"And are any of these guys still on the scene?" he asked, sounding like a prosecuting attorney browbeating a defendant.

"Oh, heavens no. None of them were from Jester."

"I s—I understand."

"Then you understand you're under absolutely no obligation to me. You're free to leave, and you'll never hear from me again."

He turned suddenly fierce. "Maybe I don't owe you anything. But I don't make it a habit to litter the countryside with my illegitimate children. So until the baby's born and you can do a DNA test, you're stuck with me."

Oh, dear. This wasn't working out at all as Gwen had planned. She thought Eli would be relieved to be given his walking papers. Certainly her father hadn't cared to stick around long enough to see his child born, and her parents had been married.

"All right," Gwen said. "If you leave me your number, I'll call you when the babies are born."

Eli's face paled. "Babies? As in, plural?"

"Twins. I just found out."

One corner of his sexy mouth turned up in a half grin. "Well, I'll be damned." But the smile quickly faded. "I don't think I trust you to call me."

"You know where to find me. Due date's October tenth. Um, Eli, suppose you are the father. What did you have in mind?'' She had a strong feeling his plans didn't include paying child support.

''A wedding, of course.'' He tipped an imaginary hat. ''I'll be seeing you.''

Gwen just stared, her mouth gaping open, as he stood and walked across her porch, down the steps and out onto the sidewalk. She watched as he walked down Main Street and climbed into his car—the classic Jaguar that had passed her on the highway earlier.

A wedding, huh? Very noble of him. For a few moments, she let herself think about that. White lace—well, maybe not white, she amended—and promises, just like the old song. Her friends around her. Cake and champagne, the bride and groom dancing. His Jaguar, painted with shoe-polish quips about the wedding night.

A honeymoon…the best part.

She sighed. That was some far-out fantasy. She might be willing to marry Eli Garrett. But the moment she mentioned the prenuptial agreement she would require, he would probably run for the hills. A prenup might seem cold, but she wasn't going to make the same mistake her mother did.

As he drove back to Denver, Eli tried not to be angry with Gwen. But he was, dammit. She'd been trying to get rid of him, and that stung.

Eli was a businessman. Among other things, he bought and sold cars, and some of the wiliest liars in the world joined him in that occupation. So Eli had gotten very good at telling when someone was lying to him.

Gwen Tanner had been lying through her pretty white teeth. For some reason she hadn't wanted him to believe he was the father of her child—children, he corrected himself.

Perhaps she just didn't want a man around. Maybe she'd approached him at The Wild Mustang for the sole purpose of getting pregnant. He'd heard of stranger things.

But that scenario didn't fit the woman he'd spent the night with. Granted, he couldn't claim to really know her after only a few hours together. But they'd connected on some elemental level. She'd been sincere that night—he was sure of it. She'd left him her number, and she'd wanted him to call.

Two explanations for her behavior occurred to him. One, she didn't want to "trap" him. Maybe she sincerely believed all that stuff she'd told him, that a man shouldn't have to be responsible for one lapse in judgment. Kind of cockeyed reasoning, but plausible.

The second possibility—that Gwen didn't want him anywhere near her money—also made sense. She didn't know him, after all. He might be some male version of a gold digger.

Neither problem was insurmountable, Eli decided, his habitual optimism coming to his rescue. Once Gwen got to know him, she would realize that he didn't want or need her money. And he would make her see that being a father wasn't some huge price he was being forced to pay. He wanted—no, insisted on—a role in his children's lives. He might not have a clue how to be a good father, but surely a clueless father was better than none at all.

Eli didn't remember either of his parents, didn't even know who they were. He'd been abandoned as an infant. But he was somewhat of an expert on foster parents. He'd lived in sixteen different foster homes during his childhood. Sometimes the surrogate parents meant well. Some had been indifferent, interested only in the money they received from the government for his care. A few were downright cruel. He'd never bonded with any of them, never kept in touch after he moved on.

He was partly to blame for that. He'd been a difficult kid with a chip on his shoulder. He'd resented the parents who had abandoned him. That resentment had fueled his ambition. Early on he'd decided to make something of himself, to prove how wrong his foolish parents had been to reject him. He'd mostly stayed out of trouble, learned a trade, started his own business and achieved success beyond his wildest dreams. But the resentment had kept everyone at arm's length.

Well, his kids weren't going to resent him. They would have to find some other motivation to succeed in life. He was going to be there, dammit.

He pressed harder on the gas, pushing the Jag to seventy-five. He had a lot to accomplish in the next couple of weeks.

THE SUMMER HEAT WAVE finally broke as September rolled around. With the high temperature only reaching the seventies, Gwen felt a renewal of her customary energy. She baked with a vengeance in her new, modern kitchen, delivering more pastries to the bookstore than the patrons could possibly eat. She tried out new recipes on her boarders and she finished the nursery—now with two of everything. Today she was serving afternoon tea on the porch. She'd bought more wicker furniture, enough to accommodate a dozen people, and she'd invited a few people over. She'd even invited Wyla Thorne. Poor Wyla—the woman was just consumed with bitterness over the fact that she'd quit the lottery pool one week too early.

As she set the wicker table with a cabbage-rose cloth and matching napkins, she counted the days and realized she hadn't heard a peep out of Eli in two weeks, which was a mixed blessing. Her rational side was sure he was attracted to her money. After all, men had never exactly flocked around her when she was slender and moderately attractive. Well, she didn't have two noses or anything. Now that she was the size of a Goodyear blimp, men ran the other way when they saw her coming.

Sylvia said it was because men got a little nervous around a pregnant woman. But Gwen suspected the men in Jester were terrified of being roped into surrogate fatherhood. It wasn't just that she was pregnant, it was that she was *single* and pregnant.

Eli had apparently come to his senses and joined the crowd. He'd probably decided her fortune wasn't worth playing dad to twins. The price was too high.

But her romantic side craved his presence. All his talk of weddings had made her skin tingle with awareness. Would he really want to marry her if he knew the twins were his? Even with a pre-nup, married to her he could still live a life of ease. For the tenth time that day, she conjured up an image of her and Eli living as husband and wife.

Gwendolyn Garrett. That was a very nice name. Although she might keep Tanner, since she couldn't change the name of the boardinghouse. That would be an insult to her grandmother.

"Yoo-hoo, hi, Gwen!"

Her fantasy bubble burst, Gwen looked up to see Mary Kay Thompson waving at her from the yard next door. Mary Kay dabbled in real estate sales, though Jester wasn't exactly a hotbed of activity in that industry.

"Guess what?" Mary Kay called out. "I finally sold this house!" She made a show of hanging a SOLD! placard on the bottom of the fading For Sale sign.

"That's great!" Gwen called back. "Who bought it?"

"Some guy from out of town." Mary Kay minced over in her high heels and joined Gwen on the porch. "And I've got something for you."

"Not another offer."

"'Fraid so." She reached into her voluminous,

flowered purse and produced a thick manila envelope, handing it to Gwen.

Gwen tucked it into her apron. "Thanks, Mary Kay. But I'm not selling."

"I wouldn't, either," Mary Kay gushed. "Not that I wouldn't mind the commission, but you've got the prettiest house in town, now that it's all fixed up."

"Thanks. Will you stay for tea?"

"No, I need to get home to Pumpkin. He suffers from separation anxiety when I'm gone. Dr. Hartman gave me a prescription to calm Pumpkin's nerves, but I still worry about him."

In Gwen's opinion, Mary Kay was the one who needed the prescription. All Pumpkin, her fat orange barn cat, needed was to live a normal cat life. Sometimes Mary Kay took the cat, which she claimed was some rare breed of Persian, on walks around town wearing a pink rhinestone collar and matching leash.

"Thanks, anyway," Mary Kay said, fluffing her permed blond hair. "Your new neighbor should be moving in right away. Keep an eye out and let me know, huh? I didn't meet him, but he sounded cute over the phone. And he's single." She turned and tiptoed down the steps, hips wiggling beneath her short, red skirt, blond hair sprayed helmet-stiff.

Gwen smiled and shook her head. Amanda always joked that Mary Kay was *ragingly* single. She'd made a play for Jack Hartman, the vet, bringing Pumpkin to him at least once a week with a new, imaginary illness. That was before Jack and Melinda, his partner, had announced their engagement.

As four o'clock approached, Gwen's guests began arriving. Stella and Irene had dressed for the occasion in pretty dresses. They were both so dear to humor her.

"This is so nice," Irene Caldwell said, fingering the tablecloth. Irene had been a widow for ten years, and had lived at Tanner's for six. She was quiet, had no children and generally conducted herself in a dignified manner. Her only indulgence was Benny, her aging Welsh corgi. Though Gwen's grandmother hadn't allowed pets, Gwen had made an exception for Benny, who was very sweet and well behaved. Besides, Irene would never have moved in without her dog, which her husband had adored. The little tan dog was twelve now but still going strong, and Gwen found she liked having him around. He was a good watchdog.

Benny had come to the porch with Irene, and now found a prime spot under the table from which he could scarf crumbs when they fell.

The other guests trickled in. Oggie arrived home from school and brought Olivia Mason with him. Olivia was a popular teacher and, with her husband, Kyle, another of the lottery winners. Gwen had also invited Jennifer Faulkner McNeil, who'd moved to Jester only recently, though she'd spent summers here with her grandparents when she was a kid. She'd returned when her grandfather died and left her his lottery winnings. Then she'd up and married Luke McNeil, the sheriff. She arrived with Vickie McNeil Perkins, her best friend and sister-in-law.

"Did anyone see Honor on her way over?" Gwen asked. Honor Lassiter was co-owner of The Mercantile with Ruby Cade. But since they'd hired teenage single mom Valerie Simms as a manager at the store, both partners had more free time. Honor had assured Gwen she would come over today.

"You must not have heard," Jennifer said. "Honor left on a round-the-world trip."

There was a murmur of surprise from those who hadn't heard the latest news, Gwen included.

"That was pretty sudden," Gwen said. "I know she's been a bit restless since she received her lottery winnings, but I didn't think she'd just up and leave. When is she coming back?"

Jennifer shrugged. "No one knows."

Gwen thought that was rather strange behavior for Honor, who was a sweet, hometown girl who'd never traveled anyplace before.

Wyla was last to arrive, though Gwen wasn't sure why she bothered. She wouldn't touch the sweets. She was paranoid about adding a single pound to her painfully thin figure.

Gwen forced herself to be pleasant, since the woman was Stella's friend. "Hello, Wyla, glad you could join us."

"Hello, Gwen. Say, I hear you cornered the fella that put the bun in your oven."

Gwen almost dropped the teapot. "What?"

"Wyla, really," Stella scolded.

"Well I'm just repeating what I've heard. He showed up at the café a couple of weeks ago," she

continued, addressing everyone, assuming they
wanted to hear gossip, "then followed Gwen to the
boardinghouse. They talked here on this very porch
before he finally took off like a scalded cat. Who else
would he be but the mystery man?"

"He could be Gwen's cousin," Jennifer spoke up.
"Or a potential boarder. He could be anyone!"

"Gwen doesn't have any cousins," Wyla said. She
looked at Gwen. "I knew both your parents, don't
forget."

"Wyla, for heaven's sake, stop badgering her,"
Irene broke in. "If Gwen wants to tell us who her
visitor is, she'll tell us." But Gwen could see Irene
was brimming with curiosity, though she was too polite to voice it.

Shoot. If Wyla knew about Eli's visit, the whole
town knew. Shelly wouldn't have said anything. But
those old men who hung out at the barbershop were
the worst gossips in town.

Gwen sank into a chair. Stella, looking sympathetic, took the teapot from her and assumed the du-
ties of hostess, pouring tea and passing around the
pastries.

"I guess it won't hurt to tell you," Gwen said.
"The man is Eli Garrett, and he's the father of my
babies. But I doubt you'll be seeing him again."

Oggie nearly came out of his chair. "He abandoned
you?" Oggie didn't mind hanging out with the ladies.
He was secure in his masculinity, and besides, he
would never turn down an opportunity to be near

Stella. But at this moment he looked furious, doing a pretty good imitation of an outraged father figure.

"He didn't exactly abandon me," Gwen said soothingly. "It was more of a mutual agreement."

"He's still a yellow dog," Oggie grumbled, reclaiming his chair. "If you were my daughter, I'd get out my shotgun and there'd be a wedding!"

Gwen didn't believe for a second that Oggie had ever owned a gun of any type. But she appreciated his protectiveness, even if it was misplaced.

Further conversation about her unwedded state was halted by a god-awful noise on Main Street. Everyone looked to see a huge U-Haul truck approaching.

"What in the world...?" Irene asked.

When the truck turned onto Lottery Lane and passed right in front of Gwen's house, she thought the driver looked familiar. A troubling suspicion began to build in her mind, especially when the truck stopped and backed into the driveway of the Carter place next door—the one Mary Kay had just sold.

"You have a new neighbor?" Olivia asked Gwen.

"It appears so. I'll go...welcome him." Better to face him privately than give the town, not to mention the ever-curious reporters, another bit of fodder for the grapevine.

Gwen walked as fast as she could in her present condition. The truck's driver opened his door and descended.

"Howdy, neighbor!" Eli said with a broad grin. "Are you the welcome wagon?"

## Chapter Three

Eli had seen Gwen in the throes of passion. He'd seen her sweetly shy, irritated and embarrassed. But he'd never seen her spitting mad. He liked it. Anger brought out the fire in her green eyes.

"What do you think you're doing?" she demanded. Wisps of her auburn hair escaped from a bun at the nape of her neck, flying every which way in the breeze like banners of fire.

He tossed her a lazy smile. "I'm moving in. I decided I like your little town, and I thought it might be fun to have an address on Lottery Lane."

"But…but you can't do that."

"Of course I can."

She bit her lower lip, a little less sure of her footing now. "Have you even been in that house?"

"Nope. Bought it sight unseen. But I'm sure it'll be fine. I'm good with my hands, and if it has any problems, I'll fix them right up."

For some reason, she smiled. "You have a key?"

"Right here." He jingled his key ring.

"Let's just go inside and have a look."

A sense of foreboding settled just under Eli's ribs. Mary Kay Thompson, the real estate agent who'd sold him this house, had warned him that it was in quite a shambles. No one had lived in it for two years, and the house had been in poor repair even before that. But he'd lived in some pretty crummy places in his life. His first apartment, which he shared with a married teenage couple, had featured a hole in the roof big enough to toss a basketball through.

The outside of the faded pink Victorian appeared to be sound. One broken window on the third floor could be fixed quickly enough. A few missing shingles, some peeling paint. Nothing fatal.

The front porch was missing a few boards. He offered his hand to Gwen, to help her across the uneven surface. She hesitated at first. He suspected she wouldn't have accepted his help if she hadn't been pregnant. Concern for her safety won out, and she took his hand.

Her hand felt small, soft and warm in his, like a little bird. He remembered how those hands had felt stroking his body, hesitant at first, then bolder as she'd realized the power she had over him.

*Better not go there.* He shuttered off those memories and focused on the house, his new home. The lock was rusty, but he finally managed to wrestle the door open.

He stepped inside and flipped a light switch. Nothing happened.

"Some critter probably chewed up your wiring," Gwen said, sounding almost happy.

"Oh, my God," was all Eli could think of to say as he took in the rotting carpets, peeling wallpaper and cobwebs. Wasps had built nests in the chandelier. Ivy grew through cracks in the windows. In the dining room, the ceiling had caved in, and it smelled as if a colony of stray cats had taken up residence.

The kitchen was even worse. The appliances were circa 1940. Even if the stove worked, he wouldn't want to use it for fear of asphyxiating himself or causing an explosion.

"Hell, I can't live here," he said, disgusted.

"Glad that's settled."

"Is Mac's Auto Repair in the same shape?"

"I don't know. Why?"

"I bought that, too." The mechanic's shop, which faced Main Street, backed up to his property. It was a perfect setup for his business. "I'm a mechanic," he explained.

"Really?" Her irritation with him fled, at least for the moment. "We haven't had a real mechanic in Jester for years."

"What about Tex's Garage?" He'd noticed the small gas station with one car bay on his way into town.

"Tex mostly works on farm equipment. He can manage a quick oil change, but if there's anything seriously wrong with a car, we have to drive or be towed to Pine Run to have it fixed. But I don't know that there would be enough business here for you to make a living. That's why Mac closed up and left."

"I'll manage."

She narrowed her eyes, her momentary affability vanished. "We'll see about that. Shall we check upstairs?"

He didn't see the point. He couldn't live here until he did some work. "I don't suppose you have a vacancy at the boardinghouse?"

"No, I'm all full." She wouldn't meet his gaze, so he kept staring at her. "Oh, all right, I do have an empty room. But you can't stay with me. What would people say?"

"You don't rent to male boarders?"

"Well, yes, I do. Oggie Lewis has been with me forever. But everybody knows—thinks you're the father of my babies. The gossips have been going nuts ever since your first visit to town."

"Then I suggest everyone will think I'm here to look after the welfare of my children. And is that so bad?"

She sighed. "But what if they're not your children?"

He sighed right back at her. "Gwendolyn, we both know they're mine. So why don't we stop pretending?"

He wasn't sure what reaction he expected, but it wasn't fear. Yet she looked up at him with huge green eyes, and that's what he saw.

"You're not...I mean, you don't want them, do you? You aren't thinking of a custody battle or something like that, are you? Because if you are, mister, you're in for a helluva—"

"Whoa, whoa, whoa. Did I say anything about custody?"

"No," she admitted.

"I wouldn't do that. I wouldn't rip two innocent children away from their mother. What kind of monster do you think I am?"

Her voice softened. "I don't think you're a monster. But I don't know you very well."

"I'd like to remedy that." His finger traced her jawline, and she didn't flinch from his touch. He thought about mentioning marriage again. But clearly Gwen was feeling vulnerable right now. If he pushed again, she might close up to him completely. He'd settle for moving into her boardinghouse—for now. "So how about you show me that empty room."

"It's not much," she admitted. "It's the smallest room in the house. I usually stick Harvey Brinkman in there when he comes to town."

"Who?"

"Harvey Brinkman. He's a reporter from the *Pine Run Plain Talker,* a real pill. He took up residence in Jester after the lottery win. Thought I'd never get rid of him. Anyway, the room is small, but it has a little sitting area and a private bath. No shower, though, just a clawfoot tub."

"Sounds fine."

"You probably don't like dogs. Irene, one of my permanent boarders, has a little Welsh corgi, and you have to be nice to him. Rules of the house."

"I don't mind dogs at all. In fact, I had one until recently."

Her face clouded. "What happened to it?"

He shrugged. "Old age." It still hurt a bit, thinking of Shadow. The big mutt had showed up at the garage, and after a couple of days Eli had been unable to resist those sad eyes and had started feeding him. Next thing he knew, he was hauling the beast to the vet, and Shadow was his. He'd kept Eli company during the day, and guarded the garage at night. He'd died last year.

A noise at the front door snagged their attention. "Yoo-hoo. Gwen? Did you fall down a rabbit hole?"

"We're in the kitchen, Stella," Gwen called. "But don't bother coming in, we're coming out."

When they emerged into the welcome daylight, Eli saw the woman belonging to the voice. She was a cute, pudgy lady in her fifties with curly blond hair and a friendly smile.

"Eli, this is Stella Montgomery. Stella, meet our new boarder."

Eli shook Stella's hand. "Just temporary, until I get my place fixed up."

"How nice to meet you," Stella effused. "Will you join us for tea? I know Oggie would enjoy having another rooster at the hen party." She tittered at her own bon mot.

"Thanks, but I have a lot to do." He had to get that truck unloaded somewhere, which meant he had to find someone to help him. "Do you ladies know of a strong man who might be looking to earn some extra money? Oh, what am I thinking? Nobody in Jester needs money."

"Don't believe everything you read in the paper," Gwen said.

"Ask Oggie how to get in touch with Jimmy—he's custodian at the school," Stella said helpfully. "Oggie's another of your neighbors and the school vice principal. I'll introduce you."

GWEN SHOWED Eli his room, which he found satisfactory. She introduced him to Oggie, who grudgingly gave him Jimmy's phone number.

After Eli left to take care of things, Gwen rejoined her guests on the porch. They all stared at her expectantly, dying to know the whole story.

She wouldn't give them the satisfaction, she decided. Only Sylvia knew she'd picked Eli up in a bar and had known him precisely ninety minutes before she'd slept with him, and Sylvia would never tell.

"We won't be seeing him again, huh?" Wyla said, enjoying the fact she could throw Gwen's words back at her. "Apparently he has other ideas. Why's he here? Is he going to make an honest woman out of you?"

"We're not getting married," Gwen said flatly.

"Why not?" Oggie wanted to know. "I'll have a talk with that young man."

"Oh, Oggie, you're a dear, but I wish you wouldn't. I believe Eli would marry me if that's what I wanted. But it's not necessary in this day and age. Single women raise children all the time. When I marry, it will be for love."

Wyla sniffed. "Good luck finding a husband when

you're a single mom. You have a better chance of…''
She paused.

''Winning the lottery!'' Jennifer finished for her,
laughter bubbling up.

Everyone else laughed, diffusing the tension. Conversation thankfully turned to other topics—like
whether Shelly was carrying a boy or a girl.

But Gwen couldn't help thinking about Wyla's
barb. She probably *wouldn't* ever get married. Even
before she was pregnant, the men hadn't exactly
flocked around her. She was just too darn shy, and
she spent any free time she had down at Pop's Movie
Theater, escaping into her favorite pastime—alone.

It was true—single mothers had a hard time of it
in the marriage department. Was she foolish to dis-
miss Eli as potential husband material?

Then again, he hadn't exactly asked her. Oh, he'd
mentioned a wedding as a toss-off line as he was leaving town two weeks ago, but she had no idea whether
he would seriously consider the possibility. Especially
if he knew he couldn't touch her money.

AFTER TWO DAYS of living under the same roof as Eli
Garrett, Gwen began to wonder exactly how he made
his living. He claimed to be a mechanic. But he'd
made no move to reopen Mac's Auto Repair to the
public. He had a couple of cars over there, rusty old
heaps that would look right at home in a junkyard.
He tinkered on them early in the morning for a couple
of hours, then worked on his house, which at this

stage consisted mostly of hauling debris out to the street.

She was ashamed to admit she'd made it her business to find out how he spent his time. She had a perfect view of his house out her kitchen window, or from the front porch. And if she wanted to get a bird's-eye view of Mac's, she went up to her apartment on the third floor and peeked out her sitting room window. Climbing all those stairs was a feat in her condition, so when she'd done it for the third time that day, she knew her interest was excessive.

But why shouldn't she be interested in the father of her children? She wanted to know what kind of genetics she was dealing with, she reasoned.

On the morning of the third day, she was out in front of her house watering her geraniums and enjoying the view—Eli moving back and forth from his house to the street, hauling crumbled plaster and rotting lumber in a wheelbarrow. Wearing old cut-off shorts and a white T-shirt, he was even more intriguing than he'd been in khakis. He had terrific legs, hard and tanned, with well-defined muscles and a dusting of dark hair.

She remembered how that rough hair had felt rubbing against her legs. And his beard, just starting to scratch after a day's growth, brushing lightly against her thigh—

"Gwendolyn!"

She gasped and whirled around, very nearly dousing the mayor with her hose. He jumped out of the way with more agility than a man of his girth should exhibit. Then again, she shouldn't be throwing stones where girth was concerned.

"Goodness, you were a million miles away," Mayor Bobby Larson said in his most unctuous tone. His blond-bimbo secretary, Paula Pratt, stood right behind him, steno-book poised to record his every brilliant word, should he give her an order. Paula's eggplant P.T. Cruiser was parked at the curb. Like they couldn't walk from the town hall? It was all of two blocks.

Not that Gwen herself would walk two blocks she didn't have to, but she had a good excuse.

"To what do I owe the honor, Mayor?" Gwen asked pleasantly, though she already knew the answer. He was going to try to get her support for the hotel. She'd been one of the most strident protesters, attending every town council meeting and pointing out all the drawbacks. Shy as she was, on this matter she was adamant, and she forced herself to speak up.

She wasn't in the mood to argue with Bobby today. Then again, as hot and bothered as she was from watching Eli, maybe a distracting argument with the mayor would help burn off some nervous energy.

Or maybe she should just turn the hose on herself.

"I hear you got another offer on your little estate, here."

"How did you know that?" She'd opened the envelope, glanced at the offer, then put it on her desk in the office and forgot about it. She hadn't spoken of it to anyone. "I hope Mary Kay Thompson knows that real estate transactions are confidential."

Bobby shrugged. "Oh, I just heard it through the grapevine. You know how Jester is."

*Yeah, right.*

"Are you considering the offer?" he asked.

"Are you trying to get rid of me?" she countered. "I know I've been a thorn in your side lately."

Bobby smiled his used-car-salesman smile. "Gwen, of course not. I'm asking out of concern. Since you'll soon have children to raise—twins, right?"

"Yes."

"Then you'll really have your hands full. Running this boardinghouse has got to be a full-time job—cooking, cleaning, laundry, yard work. How can you expect to adequately care for your children under those circumstances?"

"The same way busy women have done it for centuries, I imagine," she said mildly. "Any other questions?"

"I understand the price offered was way above the property's current valuation."

"That doesn't really matter to me," Gwen said. "I don't need the money."

"Yes, throw it in our faces, why don't you," Paula muttered.

Bobby gave his secretary a nasty look, then turned back to Gwen, ready with another argument. "I understand the, um, father of your children has come calling. Now that you're, er, reconciled, won't you be wanting to marry him and move to wherever he lives?"

"I would never leave Jester," Gwen said flatly. She hated big cities. Her maternal grandparents lived in Billings, and she occasionally visited them, though they considered her something of an embarrassment, a reminder that their daughter married a pig farmer. But they tolerated her. Other than that, Gwen never visited any cities bigger than Pine Run.

"Then he'll come here," Bobby continued. "And your third-floor apartment is too small for a family of four."

Gwen had lost patience with the meddling mayor. "I will manage somehow, thank you very much. Is this really any of your business?"

"I'm concerned," he said again. "Once the hotel project goes through, it could have a negative impact on the value of your property."

"Not to mention my quality of life," Gwen snapped. "Anyway, I thought the town council had vetoed your idea to build a hotel in the community park."

"They did. But they're beginning to come around. And there's also the Carter place. And Mac's."

"Oh, really?"

Just then, Eli dumped another wheelbarrow full of debris onto the growing pile at the curb.

Bobby looked over. "Who the devil is that?"

Gwen was surprised Bobby hadn't heard about Eli moving into the Carter place, the way gossip traveled in this town. "I'm afraid you're a little late. Eli Garrett just bought the Carter house *and* Mac's Auto Repair."

Bobby's florid face turned pale. "Th-that can't be! Those properties were going on the auction block next month. I was going to scoop them up for back taxes!"

Ah, suddenly things became clear. "Are *you* the one who's been trying to buy my house?" But of course, he was. The three properties combined—hers, the Carter place and the garage—would provide enough acreage for a small hotel, and in a prime location.

The mayor's silence was telling. That sneaky weasel!

"You want to tear down two beautiful Victorian houses for a hotel?" she persisted. She shuddered to think about it. Though Eli's appearance in her life had put a kink in her carefully laid plans for the future, she was secretly pleased he would be saving another bit of Jester's heritage.

Instead of sticking around to argue further, Bobby turned his attention to the activities next door. "Here, now!" he called to Eli. He marched toward Eli's property, Gwen forgotten. Paula trotted after him. "You can't dump all that trash in the street. We have ordinances!"

Gwen couldn't resist the urge to follow the mayor over and listen to the exchange between the two men.

Eli introduced himself and shook hands with the mayor, who clearly wasn't pleased at being forced to be cordial.

"I believe the ordinance states that large trash can be stacked near the curb, provided it's hauled away within forty-eight hours."

The mayor turned to Paula. "Make a note to check the ordinance."

"I've hired Jimmy Jenkins over at the school to bring his dump truck over tomorrow after school and haul this stuff to the landfill."

Bobby appeared extremely perturbed. But he didn't have a good comeback. He resorted to shaking his finger in Eli's face. "You just watch your step. I've got my eye on you. Gwen Tanner is like a daughter to me. I don't take kindly to city slickers moving into *my* town and trying to horn in on our women." He glanced back at Gwen, who tried not to laugh. Finally Bobby spun on his heel and stalked back to the purple car.

"Yeah!" Paula added before following her boss.

To his credit, Eli waited until they'd driven off before bursting into laughter. "That's your mayor?"

"*Our* mayor," Gwen corrected him. "No one really likes him. But his father was mayor, a good one, so no one will run against Bobby—out of respect for his dad, I guess. He's a buffoon, but you don't want him as your enemy. He can be petty and vindictive. You can bet he'll have Paula poring over all the city ordinances, trying to find a violation on your property."

"And maybe yours, too. You gave him an earful."

"Eavesdropping, were you?"

"Didn't have to. You were pretty loud. Which surprises me. Everyone I've met refers to you as shy, sweet, quiet. You don't seem that way to me."

"Being seven-and-a-half months pregnant makes me cranky. I speak my mind more than I used to."

He winked at her. "Keep it up. You're beautiful when you're mad."

"I won't dignify that with a response." But secretly she reveled in the flirtation. He had good reason to weasel his way into her good graces, but she wanted to believe his compliments were sincere.

ONE WEEK after moving to Jester, Eli woke up in his little room in the boardinghouse, his muscles protesting vigorously. He couldn't remember the last time he'd worked this hard. Maybe it was when he was twenty-one, after his one and only brush with the Colorado legal system. That had been a wake-up call. Before that, he'd thought the way lots of kids did— that he was invincible, smarter than the authorities, and that he could beat the system and smart-mouth his way through any situation.

Well, he couldn't wiggle out of massive debt. He'd obtained credit cards—dozens of them—with amazing ease. Every time the payments would get too high, he would get another card and transfer the balances. But eventually no one would give him another card, and the "house of cards" came crashing down on him.

He remembered the exact moment he realized that the world wasn't going to give him a free ride just because he was clever and good-looking. His big plans to "be somebody" wouldn't come to fruition without hard work, and a lot of it.

That was when he'd gotten the job at Cooper's Mechanic Shop. He'd proved himself a quick study, and Old Man Coop let him work ten, twelve, sometimes fifteen hours a day. He'd started taking on special jobs, time-consuming repairs on old Mercedes and Jaguars that no one else wanted to touch. He'd reveled in tracking down exotic replacement parts, scouring junkyards for the fender to a 1965 Barracuda or tooling a special part himself.

His reputation quickly grew, and Coop, who was near retirement anyway, helped him spin off his own business specializing in classic and antique cars.

His first big break came when he recognized a rare 1916 Stutz Bearcat, rusting away in a junkyard. He bought it for almost nothing, restored it, then sold it to a collector for an obscene profit. A few more successes like that, and he'd been written up in the newspaper. The wire services had picked up the story— Orphan Grease Monkey Makes Good. Pretty soon, people from all over the country were calling him for advice, or to help them find a certain part.

He realized his vast database of knowledge, not to mention the one he kept on his computer, was worth something, and he became a consultant. When the Smithsonian Institution acquired a rare vehicle, Eli Garrett was the man they called to restore it. Sometimes he was amazed at what people would pay him—and all for doing something he loved.

The renovations to his new house had eaten into his garage time, though. He'd been neglecting the 1928 Nash, which required a never-ending list of rare parts that had to be tracked down and oddball paint colors that Eli mixed himself, recreating the manufacturer's original colors. Eli was a nut for authenticity, and so were his customers.

Eli had been putting in twelve-hour days of hard physical labor of one kind or another. No wonder he was so sore, he thought as he folded his six-foot-plus body into the small clawfoot tub. But the house was still a long way from livable.

He shouldn't be in that much of a hurry. He enjoyed living in Gwen's house, even with the cramped bathing facilities. The dinners were excellent, the company entertaining and the room comfortable, although he would much rather be living on the third floor with Gwen.

He'd never even been upstairs. He had no legitimate reason. And he was dying of curiosity. Would Gwen's quarters reflect the same good taste as the rest of the house, which featured oak floors, Oriental rugs, off-white walls and fine mahogany furnishings? Or would it be a more personal reflection of the woman herself?

As Eli dressed in jeans and a work shirt, he noticed something missing. No delicious scent of blueberry muffins or cinnamon rolls wafted into his room from the kitchen. Gwen was normally an early riser, so that she could bake her pastries for the bookstore. He was amazed how quickly he'd become accustomed to the pleasant wake-up call.

Eli emerged from his room at around seven-thirty

and found Irene and Stella dithering in the dining room.

"Oh—Gwen's not with you, then?"

"With me? No." Only in his dreams.

"The kitchen's dark and the oven cold," Stella said ominously. "We thought maybe…well, we didn't want to disturb you if…but apparently you haven't."

Eli didn't need to hear anymore. He headed straight up the stairs.

"Gwen is very protective of her privacy," Irene called after him.

He didn't care. She might be in trouble. She just wasn't the type to sleep late on a Monday morning. A sign on the second-floor landing at the foot of Gwen's staircase—Private—didn't deter him. He climbed the narrow, twisting staircase, arriving at Gwen's door.

He knocked, hard. "Gwen? Are you in there?"

"Uh, just a minute." He was relieved to hear her voice, but troubled by its raspy quality. A few moments later, Gwen cracked the door open. "What are you doing here?" she asked crossly.

"I was worried about you. You're always up by six."

"Well, what time is it?" She looked at her watch and gasped. "Oh, my stars! How did that happen?" She turned away from the door without shutting it, so Eli took the opportunity to push his way in.

He gave the apartment only scant attention, noticing only that it wasn't like the rest of the house. It was more like—a harem, with hanging silks, bright colors, huge pillows on the floor. But he was more focused on Gwen, who wore a Chinese red silk robe. She'd been heading for what he presumed was her bedroom, but she'd stopped with her hand on the knob, eyes closed. She wavered slightly on her feet, and Eli jumped to support her in case she fell.

She looked awful. Beautiful, but awful. No doubt about it, she was sick.

He put a hand to her forehead. It was burning up.

"You're going to the doctor."

"It's just a little flu. I called Doc Perkins last night and he sent over a prescription."

"Is it safe for you to take medicine? For the babies, I mean?"

"It's okay to take some things. Don't worry, Nathan Perkins is a great doctor. I'm sure he took my pregnancy into account."

"Yeah, well, whatever he gave you isn't working. You're sick as a dog."

"I'll be fine," she insisted. "Just let me get to the shower."

"You're not going anywhere except a doctor's office. If you won't think of your own health, think of the twins."

That did it. She slumped against him, all her fight gone. "Let me put some clothes on." But in the end she couldn't even do that, she was too weak. So Eli scooped her up and carried her down the stairs.

## Chapter Four

Gwen had never felt so humiliated. "Please, put me down," she begged. "I'm going to give you a hernia. Worse yet, you'll lose your footing going down these stairs and kill us both."

"Hush up," Eli said.

So she did. She closed her eyes and cuddled up against Eli's massive chest, feeling suddenly safe and protected. She hadn't felt that way since her grandmother died ten years ago. She was so used to taking care of herself and her guests, she'd forgotten what it was like to just surrender and let someone else take control.

"Oh, my heavens, what's wrong?" she heard Irene ask.

"I'm not sure," Eli said. "She's weak and feverish, and in her condition I'm not taking any chances. Do either of you have a car?"

"Mine's parked out back," Stella answered quickly. "This way. The clinic is just down the block."

"Is it open this early?"

"Oh, yes," Irene assured him. "Doc Perkins opens early for the convenience of folks who'd like to come in before work."

"Never mind the car, then. I'll carry her."

Gwen wanted to object, but she was too sick to care much that everybody in town would see Eli carrying her down the street in her Chinese silk robe.

At the last minute, Stella took the afghan she'd been crocheting, which was almost completed, and tossed it over Gwen. "Don't want you catching a chill on top of everything else."

Stella led Eli to the Jester Medical Center, which was mercifully close, and hurried to open the door.

"Oh, heaven help us!" Gwen recognized the voice of Carlie Goodwin, the clinic's new receptionist. She was a sweet, grandmotherly type who'd been hired after the last receptionist had gone off to college. Carlie was tailor-made for this job. She took each case to heart and made everyone feel like they could have been her own children or grandchildren. Whether it was the sniffles or something more serious, Carlie's personal concern was always a balm to any patient who crossed the threshold. "Is she in labor?"

"Just the flu," Gwen murmured as Eli set her gently on one of the comfy waiting-room sofas. Dr. Nathan Perkins was also one of the lottery winners. He'd used some of his winnings to spiff up the clinic, which was now decorated in plush fabrics and soothing earth tones.

"Doc Perkins is out on a call, but Dr. O'Rourke is

here,'' Carlie explained. ''He's with a patient right now, but he can see you soon as he's done.''

Gwen would rather have seen Doc Perkins, who'd been Jester's doctor for the past several years, ever since graduating from medical school. He wasn't much older than Gwen herself, but with his prematurely gray hair, he seemed older.

Still, she didn't want to wait. She wanted to get this ordeal over with, so she could go home and hibernate until the whole incident became nothing more than a bad dream.

''You'll love Dr. O'Rourke,'' Carlie said, as if sensing Gwen's hesitancy. ''He's really good with the kids.''

''Of course I'll see Dr. O'Rourke,'' Gwen said, feeling silly. Young, good-looking doctors made her nervous. But Conner was married to Shelly, after all. It wasn't as if he was a stranger.

While they waited, Eli sat next to her, watching her like a cat with a mouse—a sick mouse, she amended. Irene and Stella sat across from her in matching wingback chairs, also studying her.

''You all don't have to wait,'' she said. ''In fact, Stella, it would be a big help if you could bring your car over so I don't have to parade down Lottery Lane half-dressed when I get done here. And Irene, I'd really appreciate it if you could stay at the house. We left it empty and the front door wide open. Besides, I'm expecting a call from a potential boarder.'' It wasn't exactly a lie. She was always expecting a call from a potential boarder. ''And Eli—''

"I'm staying right here."

She didn't get a chance to argue further. Valerie Simms entered the waiting room from the treatment area, baby Max in her arms. Valerie had moved to Jester shortly after hearing about the lottery win. Alone and destitute, she'd left Max in a carrier on the counter at The Brimming Cup, believing Shelly would be a good mother to him. In the end, though, she'd realized she couldn't give up her child and had reclaimed him. The whole town had sort of adopted Val and Max. She had a job now managing The Mercantile, and she was dating Seth Hollis, whose grandfather Finn was one of the Main Street Millionaires.

"Came through his checkup like a champion, I'll bet," Carlie said to Val as she prepared a bill on her new computer.

"Healthy as a horse," Val confirmed. "But Ms. Tanner, you don't look so hot."

"Flu," she murmured, wishing Val would call her Gwen like everyone else. She was only a few years older than Val. Being "Ms. Tanner" made her feel like her grandmother. "I'm probably contagious," she added. "Don't let Max anywhere near me."

"There's something going around," Val said, looking sympathetic. "Hope you're better soon." She tore out a check and handed it to Carlie. "Oh, Eli, those work boots you wanted came in yesterday afternoon. I was going to call you when I got back to the store."

"I'll pick them up later, thanks."

Gwen had never seen anyone blossom like Val had. Once she'd made a commitment to motherhood, everything had fallen into place for her. She seemed to be juggling her many responsibilities with grace and competence.

Gwen hoped it would work that way for her, too. Right now, *grace* and *competence* didn't belong in the same room with her.

Connor O'Rourke appeared at the waiting room door. "You can come on back, Gwen."

Easier said than done. Eli had to help her to her feet. "Doc Perkins shouldn't have bought such squishy furniture," she grumbled, though secretly she enjoyed the feel of Eli's strong hands grasping her own.

Eli started to follow her back to the treatment area, but she gave him a look that stopped him cold. No way was he invited to the exam room, no matter how concerned he was for his unborn children.

The exam room featured a mural of purple elephants and blue giraffes. Connor *was* a pediatrician, but in a small town like Jester, he was required to do a bit of everything.

He bantered with her while he conducted his examination. After a few nervous minutes, Gwen relaxed. He was utterly professional, completely reassuring, just as she'd heard. Besides, he was Shelly's husband, and Shelly wouldn't marry a jerk.

"So?" Gwen asked as he pulled off his gloves and washed his hands. "Can you give me a shot or something? I've been taking my prenatal vitamins, but maybe I need something extra."

"Gwen, I hate to tell you this, but you need to go to the hospital."

"What? No, oh, Connor, no, please. Don't make me do that. I'm not that sick…am I?"

"You've got a high fever and you're seriously dehydrated. That's bad enough under any circumstances, but you're also dealing with a high-risk pregnancy. I'll call All Saints in Pine Run and let them know you're coming. Who's your obstetrician?"

Resigned to her fate, she glumly gave him the information he needed. Then she forced her trembling legs to take her to the waiting room, where she delivered the bad news.

The expression on Eli's face could only be described as stricken. "What's wrong?"

She shrugged, repeating what Connor had told her. "I'm sure it's nothing serious. Putting me in the hospital is just a safety precaution because of the pregnancy." She turned to Stella. "Do you have time to take me to Pine Run?"

"I'll take you," Eli said decisively. "You need someone strong to help you from the car."

"He's right," Stella said, handing Eli her keys. "Here, take my car, it's right out front. And Gwen, don't worry about a thing. We'll all pitch in at the boardinghouse to keep things running smoothly."

"You're…you're not coming with us?"

"Since you're under the weather, I have to think about dinner," Stella said briskly. "I'm sure Eli will take care of you." She winked as she made a quick exit from the clinic.

Even through her fever haze, Gwen saw what was going on. Stella was such a happy person, and though she'd lost her Prince Charming, she wanted everyone else to pair up and live happily ever after.

Gwen mentally balked at the idea of Eli checking her into the hospital. This was all much too personal. Eli was her fantasy lover. Memories of their perfect, passionate encounter kept her going when her back hurt and she had three loads of laundry ahead of her. Whatever idealized memories Eli might have of their night in his hotel room would surely be obliterated if he spent too much time with her in this condition.

But she couldn't shake him off, no matter how much she protested. He drove her to Pine Run. He half carried her into the hospital, dealt with the inevitable red tape of forms to fill out, waited while she saw her obstetrician, who'd come to admit her, and waited some more while her room was readied. He bought her some ginger ale, which she forced herself to drink.

"Why are you doing this?" she asked, probably too abruptly, but she was too sick to make the effort to be tactful.

"Doing what?"

"Taking all this trouble."

"Someone has to. I know you like being self-sufficient, but everybody needs help at one time or another. This is your time."

"Yes, but Stella could have handled this. She and Irene have been mothering me since my grandmother died. Sometimes I think that's why they both moved into Tanner's.''

''Where's your real mother?''

''She died when I was a baby, and quit changing the subject. You're being too nice, especially since I haven't been particularly nice to you.'' She'd been cordial, but not gracious. Friendly, but cool. She simply couldn't quell her suspicions about Eli Garrett. If only he'd showed up in her life *before* she'd become a millionaire.

Sometimes she wished she'd never won the damn money.

''I'm concerned about you and the babies,'' Eli said evenly. ''That's all.''

''Shouldn't you be worried about your business? Lots of people are anxious for you to reopen Mac's.''

He gave her a blank look. ''Where did they get the idea I'm reopening Mac's?''

''Well, you're a mechanic, aren't you?''

''Yes, but I'm very…specialized.''

He didn't elaborate, which only fueled Gwen's suspicions. Why didn't he just tell her exactly how he made his living?

She was able to escape Eli's overwhelming presence a few minutes later when an orderly took her to her private room. She'd told Eli to go on home, and she assumed he did.

As intravenous fluids poured into Gwen's body, and her fever came down, she started feeling better. She was positively euphoric when her obstetrician reported that her babies were fine, no sign that her illness was affecting them.

That euphoria lasted only until the door opened and Eli reappeared. She was instantly aware of the fact that she wore only a thin hospital gown, and that she was buck naked beneath it. She pulled the covers up in an instinctual gesture.

"What are you doing here?" she asked, wishing she didn't sound so peevish. "I thought you'd gone home."

"I went back long enough to return Stella's car. And I brought some things for you." He set an overnight case at the foot of her bed.

"You packed a bag?" The thought of Eli going through her dresser drawers was unsettling, to say the least.

"Stella did it. I brought you this." He had a plastic grocery sack in his other hand, which he set on her tray table. Something smelled good. He reached into the bag and carefully extracted a container full of chicken soup.

He smiled. "It's still warm."

"Stella didn't make it, did she?" Gwen asked warily.

"No. I picked it up at The Brimming Cup. Dan is quite a good cook, I understand."

"Yeah, if you can stand his attitude." Dan Bertram was Shelly's cook, had been since forever. His grumpy temper was legendary. But Eli was right, the man could cook, and Shelly insisted he had a compassionate, intelligent side. "He even bakes a pretty good pie. But mine are better."

Eli patted his trim stomach. "I know. I'm going to get fat if you keep feeding me those éclairs."

Gwen tried not to think about his trim stomach or anything else in that general area. She instead focused on the soup, which was pretty tasty. "I read about this man whose wife fed him soup while he was in the hospital. The soup was laced with arsenic. He died right there in the hospital, and no one figured it out for months."

"Well that's a helluva thing to say."

She laughed. "I'm eating the soup, aren't I?"

Eli scowled at her, but he showed no signs of leaving. "You must be feeling better."

"A little. I'll probably get to go home tomorrow or the next day."

"Don't think you're going to resume your previous schedule. You need to rest."

"Why thank you, Dr. Garrett, but I think I can determine the appropriate level of rest myself."

"I'm serious, Gwen. You try to do too much. If you won't hire someone to help you, then at least let the rest of us help you out. We can take turns cooking and doing laundry."

"And sweeping the floor and watering the flowers, don't forget that."

"We can handle all of that. Stella, Irene and I already talked about it. You get to sit on the porch with your feet up."

"You?" She had a hard time picturing Eli in an

apron, taking a pot roast out of the oven or wielding a broom. It was easier to picture him chopping down huge trees or digging a foundation for a skyscraper.

"I know how to cook and clean. Certainly no one else has ever done those things for me, except you. Really, you're being a complete sexist."

Her ears perked up. That was the first hint about his past that he'd dropped. "What about your mother?"

He sighed. "That's something we have in common. No mother. And the less said about that, the better."

Well, so much for the crack in his armor. Still, it was one tiny piece of information. If she worked at it, maybe he would give her more, and she could piece together a history.

Her children would want to know about their father, even if he was long gone by the time they became curious.

TWO DAYS LATER, Eli arrived at All Saints to take Gwen home. She was waiting on a bench near the front entrance. Even from a distance, Eli could tell she was much better. Her hair was back in its customary bun. She was neatly dressed in a denim jumper and olive-green turtleneck shirt, holding a large potted plant in what was left of her lap. As he drew closer, he could see roses in her cheeks and a sparkle in her eye.

She must have a robust nature if a couple of days rest and lots of fluids could cause her to bounce back so quickly from her illness. But he intended to make sure she didn't neglect her health again, even if he had to tie her to her easy chair and force herbal tea down her.

She didn't realize he was there until he pulled his car up right next to her and rolled down the window. "Hiya, lady. Goin' my way?"

For a few moments she just stared at the car he was driving. He'd actually managed to get the old Nash's engine running. The car had needed a spin on a long stretch of highway to blow all the crud out of its pipes, so when Stella had complained of a headache and had asked Eli to take Gwen home from the hospital for her, he'd readily agreed. The car's interior was a disaster and the heater didn't work, but the weather was mild, and he'd brought a huge fluffy quilt Gwen could keep cozy in, just in case she felt chilly.

Gwen put the plant on the ground, then stood and gave the car a good once-over. "What are you doing here in this…this contraption?"

"This, Gwendolyn, is a classic. It might not look like much yet, but give me a little more time and you'll be begging me to take you for a spin."

"I doubt that. Where's Stella?"

"She has a headache and asked me to come in her place." He climbed out of the car, which he left idling so it wouldn't stall on him, and grabbed Gwen's overnight case and the plant. Since the Nash had a rumble seat where the trunk ought to be, he wedged Gwen's things behind the seats.

"Stella has never had a headache in her life," Gwen said. "What's the deal?"

Eli shrugged. "All I know is, she asked me to bring you home."

*Home.* He liked the sound of that word. He'd lived in The Tanner Boardinghouse scarcely a week, but already it felt like more of a home than any place he'd ever lived. Even the house he was restoring for himself lacked a certain warmth.

There was a sense of community in Gwen's rambling Victorian. Even Jester was starting to feel like home. Though he sensed it would be a long time before he earned the close-knit town's trust, most people were gracious to him and willing to give him the benefit of the doubt.

Except the mayor. Eli wasn't sure what the full story was there, but Bobby Larson seemed to go out of his way to make life unpleasant for Eli.

"I guess I'm stuck with you, huh," Gwen said as Eli offered his arm for support. But she gave him a crooked smile, and Eli's heart soared. Earning smiles from Gwen had become of tantamount importance to him. He realized she didn't trust him, and he didn't blame her. When a man slept with a woman, then failed to call when he promised he would, well, that was pretty bad. He had a long, uphill climb to convince her he was sincere, and that he truly wanted to take responsibility for the children he'd sired simply because it was the right thing to do.

He was still wildly attracted to her, but she

wouldn't believe that, either. He would have to show her—when the time was right.

With Gwen tucked snugly into the passenger seat and buckled in, Eli took off for Jester. The engine sputtered a couple of times, earning suspicious glares from Gwen, but soon it was purring smoothly down Route 2. The eerily barren landscape that rolled past their windows was oddly beautiful. Nothing like an early fall day in the Northwest.

"So this is what you mean by specialized?" Gwen asked. "You restore old cars?"

"Yup."

"How did you learn to do it?"

"Trial and error, mostly." He could see that his clipped answers didn't satisfy her, but he wasn't used to talking about himself. When *Fortune* magazine had sent a reporter to do a story about him, he'd been so reticent that the feature the magazine had planned had been downgraded to a single-column story. Even that small mention had gotten him more business than he could handle.

Though the public loved a "Poor Boy Makes Good" story, he preferred not to churn up his sad past. Besides the fact that he didn't care to relive those memories, he had a few skeletons in the closet that he preferred to keep under wraps.

But that was all long behind him. He wasn't the same man he'd been at twenty-one, and he didn't want to be forced to continually defend the poor choices he'd made as an overconfident kid.

"So what did your doctor say?" Eli asked, wanting

to turn the conversation away from his past. "Any instructions for when you get home?"

"I have some pills to take, and more vitamins. A little exercise, lots of rest, nutritious meals. The usual stuff."

"Did they figure out what was wrong with you?"

"Ear infection. Which was strange, since my ear didn't hurt. Or maybe I just didn't notice it, since everything hurts these days."

Poor Gwen. There were times he was really grateful to be male. He would get to enjoy the pleasures of parenthood without paying the price. Then again, he might not get to see his kids at all if Gwen's attitude toward him didn't improve.

The possibility froze him up inside. He'd meant what he told her a few days ago. He would never sue her for custody or even visitation rights. He was determined to win her over, to work this thing from the inside. He would never in a million years wrangle with Gwen over the children. Such disagreeable conditions could leave terrible marks on impressionable minds. He'd seen enough of that in foster homes to know what he was talking about.

He was confident he could win her over, with patience. One way or another, the twins were going to have two concerned and involved parents.

## Chapter Five

After two days of being pampered, Gwen was beginning to feel as spoiled as Mary Kay Thompson's cat. No one at the boardinghouse would let her lift a finger. Oggie, Irene, Stella and Eli presented a united front. Irene did all the dusting, sweeping and laundry; Stella had commandeered the kitchen. And though Stella's cooking was worse than what they served at the school cafeteria, none of the others had complained about it—a sure sign they were determined not to worry Gwen.

Oggie took care of the grass, shrubs and flower beds, and watered the many potted plants Gwen nurtured inside the house. He also seemed to think it was his sworn duty to scowl at Eli every time the two men passed each other. Oggie had made it no secret that he believed it was Eli's fault Gwen was still single. Gwen had tried to convince him this just wasn't true, but he obviously didn't believe her.

As for Eli, he did whatever tasks the others allowed him to do, which included taking out the garbage and various small fix-it projects that cropped up. Though all four of Gwen's boarders were in agreement about her need for rest, it was also clear that Eli was still an outsider, and he would be treated as such until he proved himself.

Gwen hoped "proving himself" didn't include marrying her, or poor Eli might have a long wait for acceptance.

On this third day of her "confinement," she sat on the porch, wrapped in one of Stella's afghans and reading a book borrowed from Irene, who seemed to have an endless supply of recent bestsellers. She was one of Amanda's best customers at Ex-Libris and occasionally helped Amanda part-time. This particular book was a time-travel romance, not something Gwen would ordinarily have picked up, but she was now entrenched in the pages and thinking she could really get used to this life of leisure.

She didn't realize Eli was nearby until she heard his hammer pounding away just a few feet from her. She jumped, startled. But her accelerated heartbeat had more to do with Eli's nearness than anything.

"Hey, give a girl some warning," she called out.

Eli smiled down at her from a ladder. He was nailing up a loose piece of latticework—something she'd been meaning to take care of for weeks. "Sorry, I didn't see you there. How are you feeling?"

"I'm fine," she insisted. "But I'm going into baking withdrawal." She lowered her voice. "And if I have to eat any more of Stella's casseroles I'm *really* going to be sick. I mean, come on—hot dogs, Velveeta and canned mushrooms? Can't you convince the others to at least let me resume cooking?''

Eli grinned even wider. ''I've taken care of it. Irene and Stella are trading jobs.''

''Really? How did you manage that? Stella fancies herself quite a gourmet cook, you know.''

Eli hung his hammer on his belt and moved down the ladder to perch on one of its steps. ''I suggested to Stella that it might not be quite fair, giving Irene all the disagreeable tasks like scrubbing bathrooms and such. Stella is so naturally sweet, she agreed immediately and relinquished her apron. They'll probably trade back in a couple of days, but at least we're safe from salmon loaf until then.''

Gwen didn't like laughing at Stella's expense, but she couldn't help it. Last night's salmon loaf had been just about the most repulsive dish she'd ever seen. Who ever heard of putting radishes in salmon loaf?

''Can Irene cook?'' Eli asked.

''I don't know. She never has, in the six years since she's been here. But I'm willing to take my chances. Unless, of course, you pit bulls will let me back in my own kitchen.''

''Not on your life.''

''I'm going stir-crazy!''

''Have you taken your walk today?''

''I made it once around the block, the same boring block I always walk.''

''How about walking to Pop's? Matinee prices are good until four o'clock, and he's showing a sci-fi double-feature on screen two. *Day of the Triffids* and *Night of the Lepus.*"

"Lepus. Is that the giant rabbit movie?"

Eli nodded enthusiastically. "You know it?"

Eli didn't realize it, but he'd just touched on Gwen's one and only lifetime indulgence. She'd been a movie addict since she was a child. Though she wouldn't say her childhood had been unhappy, she'd been a shy and awkward little girl. Escaping into the fictional world on the silver screen had become a passion. In that wonderful, dark old theater, with the clackety-clack of the projector and the smell of buttered popcorn all around her, Gwen could pretend she was Cleopatra, Princess Leia or even Indiana Jones. She hadn't had much time lately for her favorite time-waster, though.

"What's showing on the other screen?" she asked.

Eli scrunched up his face. "Some romance."

"Oh, I remember. That new one directed by...you know, that guy who did—"

"*Not Myself.* It's been out six months."

"That's new for Pop's." Actually, Pop had been dead for twenty years. His son Don ran the theater. In a day and time when most small-town theaters had been killed off by video rentals, Don managed to keep Pop's open by running "newer" movies on one screen and classics on the other—and serving the best popcorn in two states.

Gwen's mouth watered at the thought of that popcorn. The theater was close enough she could walk—as was just about everything in Jester. "You know, that's not a bad idea.'' She picked up the *Pine Run Plain Talker,* which she'd read earlier, and found the entertainment page. ''It starts at four. Perfect. Don't know why I didn't think of it myself.''

She pushed herself up and headed inside to get her sweater and purse, feeling Eli's gaze on the back of her neck.

She often found an excuse to make a hasty escape when Eli was around. Not that she didn't like being close to him. The problem was, she liked it too much. If he was within touching range, she found her hands itching to reach out and stroke those strong muscles or ruffle his dark hair. If he ever found out how much she still wanted him, it would be embarrassing. She couldn't imagine he would find her attractive in her current condition, and the thought of an unrequited crush was downright humiliating.

She avoided Eli for another reason. She was afraid to talk to him about the future, about the role he would play in their children's lives. She didn't want to know yet what his intentions were. If he wanted to marry her, she would have to make it clear that her small fortune was off-limits to him. And she really, really didn't know what his reaction might be.

If he *didn't* want to marry her…well, she didn't want to know that, either.

He didn't seem in any hurry to voice his intentions. Maybe he had some of the same concerns she did— that whatever he suggested wouldn't sit well with her, and they would have to mar their friendship with arguments.

They were friends, she realized. After everything he'd done for her—from the chicken soup to the handyman repairs—she couldn't think of him as less.

She wanted to think of him as more, but she was afraid to.

As she ambled along Main Street toward Pop's, she pondered why she was so timid when it came to relationships. She wished she could be more like her friend Sylvia. When Sylvia saw a man she wanted, she pounced. She wasn't afraid of rejection. She didn't worry about the future. Her relationships lasted as long as they lasted, and when they ended, there were no tears, no recriminations, no "if only I'd done things differently."

She simply moved on, savoring the good memories.

Gwen supposed her conservative upbringing with her grandmother had partly contributed to her shyness. Not a day went by that Grandmother hadn't reminded her that most men were losers, out for one thing. They used and abused women, then cast them aside without a thought. And who could blame the woman for feeling that way? Her own son had deceived, knocked up and abandoned Gwen's mother. As for Gwen's paternal grandfather, her grandmother never spoke of him. Gwen could only assume something dreadful had happened concerning their marriage, if there'd even been a marriage.

But sometimes Gwen was sure she'd just been born shy. The night she'd met Eli had been an aberration.

"One for *Not Myself,* please," she said to Don at

the ticket window. Don was large and lumbering. He hadn't finished high school, and he'd never done anything except run the theater. But he knew everything about movies, far more than Gwen herself, and for that she respected him. He was also very kind.

"Well, hello, Gwendolyn," he said warmly as he made change for her, carefully counting out the coins. "I'm not sure you'll like this one so well. It's kind of sad."

"I could use a good tearjerker." Nothing like a good cry.

"Okay, don't say I didn't warn you. If you decide you don't like it, you can sneak into the other theater and watch the big rabbits. I'll look the other way."

She smiled. "Thanks, Don."

Inside, she bought a small popcorn. Not exactly on her diet, but not forbidden, either, and she could hardly sit through a movie without popcorn, could she?

Inside the dimly lit theater, she felt the familiar anticipation come over her. She found her customary seat, the middle of the third row from the back. She had the small auditorium to herself.

For about three minutes. Then a man joined her. It took her about half a second to realize the man was Eli, and he was heading straight for her.

He sat down next to her, propped his large lemonade on his knee and helped himself to a few kernels of her popcorn. "When I suggested a movie, I meant we should go together."

"You mean, like a date?"

''Yes, like a date. Your well-meaning friends at the boardinghouse would like for us to get together, but they're so suspicious of me they won't give us a minute alone.''

''Oh. What do we need a minute alone for?'' She knew she sounded exceedingly stupid. But it was hard to think straight with that hard male body next to hers. She could smell his shampoo and laundry detergent, and the scent of fresh air. It was even more alluring than the popcorn.

''Gwen. We've been avoiding it for too long. I'd like to talk about our children.''

''You mean, like, what sports we should encourage them to play, and whether to get them piano lessons?''

''I mean, like, am I going to be a part of those decisions?''

''You're their father.''

''And you know as well as I do that I have no rights over your children unless you give them to me.''

''That's not true at all. Fathers have all kinds of rights. The courts are full of—''

''I have no intention of going to court. I don't believe in lawsuits for every occasion. I want us to work this out like mature, considerate adults.''

''What if I were to say I want to raise the twins alone?''

Eli didn't answer right away. She sensed the tension in him. Finally he spoke, his voice low and even. ''I would try to convince you otherwise. But Gwen, surely you know a child is better off with two caring parents—"

"Hold on, hold on. That was just a hypothetical situation. I don't plan to deny you access to your children."

He relaxed slightly. "So you were just yanking my chain."

Maybe she had been. "I guess I was just wanting to put the worst-case scenario out on the table. But we're not going there."

"Then where are we going?"

The $64,000 question. "What do you want? How do you see it?"

"That's two different questions. The way I see it? You'll have custody. I'll have unlimited visitation, a privilege I won't ever abuse."

"And you'll live next door?"

"Yes."

"They'll call you Dad," she said, "and everything will be open and honest. Have I got it right?"

"That's the way I see it—the most likely scenario. But it's not what I want."

"Okay, I'll bite. What do you want?"

"I want to marry you."

Gwen's heart pushed into her throat. So it hadn't been a toss-off line. He really *was* willing to marry her.

The lights dimmed and the film started. Gwen used that as an excuse not to reply, and Eli didn't push her. He settled deeper into his chair and helped himself to another handful of her popcorn.

"They sell this stuff in the lobby, you know," she whispered.

"I'm saving you from yourself. You eat this whole bag, you'll retain water for days."

"Thank you for pointing that out. You are *such* a gentleman." But she moved the bag over so he would have easier access, and he offered her frequent sips of his lemonade.

The movie was good, and Gwen tried to lose herself in it. But she couldn't quite forget about the marriage proposal on the table. Certainly this time she would have to give Eli an answer.

She wanted to say yes. Her naive, romantic side longed to throw her arms around him and drag him to the nearest preacher. But her practical side forced her to consider all aspects of the issue. Did a one-night stand and an unplanned pregnancy add up to a good reason to commit for the rest of her life to a man she barely knew?

The movie's leading actress, a young unknown, cozied up to her leading man, and Gwen couldn't help but notice how slender the actress was. Gwen used to be that size. She suspected she'd never see size four again, except in children's clothes.

Uh-oh. This was more than cozy. The characters on screen were going to make love. Gwen was used to watching movies alone. She hadn't counted on watching a sex scene with Eli sitting right beside her.

It was a scene to remember, too, for what it didn't show. The woman never showed a single part of her body that couldn't be revealed at a neighborhood

swimming pool. But the lovemaking was so beautifully choreographed, so subtle, so *sexy,* that what
wasn't revealed became as arousing as what was.

Gwen was suddenly aware that Eli had slipped an
arm around her shoulders. He idly caressed her neck
with one thumb. That single, innocent contact was all
Gwen could think about—until he leaned closer and
nibbled her ear.

She knew she should tell him to stop. But it felt so
good, her body wouldn't obey as her brain instructed.
Instead, she concentrated on what felt like a million
nerve endings in her ear and at the nape of her neck,
and recalled in delicious detail exactly what Eli was
capable of doing to the rest of her nerve endings.

Gwen ceased to be interested in how the characters
on screen were getting along. She could think of nothing except that Eli's innocent, playful gestures were
driving her wild. He probably didn't even realize he
was doing it. Surely no man in his right mind would
purposely drive a very pregnant woman insane with
a longing that couldn't be quenched.

She turned her face toward his, intending to say
something, anything, to end the torture. But his mouth
claimed hers, and the kiss was deep and wet and thoroughly delicious. His lips were slightly salty from the
popcorn.

She wrapped her arms around his shoulders, sur-
rendering. She didn't care that she was making out in
a movie theater like a lusty teenager. At least they
were the only ones here.

Eli moved one hand to her breast. Oh, how she'd

wanted this! She'd dreamed almost every night of
Eli's hands on her. She wished desperately to get rid
of the barrier of clothing between them, so she could
get the full effect, but even with her brain short-
circuited by her cravings, she was still cognizant of
their surroundings.

She thought he would suggest they move to a more
amenable location, but he didn't. He seemed content
to make out with her in the dark, with the flickering
of the film playing over them.

When the house lights came up, Gwen realized
they'd missed the end of the movie.

She broke the embrace and stared into Eli's pas-
sion-hazed eyes. "Damn," he said, his voice thick
with feigned regret. "I wanted to find out how it
ended. Now we'll have to sit through it again."

"I am not—"

He grinned. "Gotcha. How about I drive us into
Pine Run for a steak dinner?"

"Oh, I don't know. I'm not sure I'm up to it."
Actually, she was. She was feeling full of energy and
hungrier than she'd been in weeks. But a steak dinner
seemed to imply Eli might expect something special
afterward, and she didn't mean a hot-fudge sundae.

"What would you like to do, then?" he asked,
seemingly unfazed by her turndown.

*Go home and make love.* But really, that was out
of the question. Though technically there was no
medical reason a pregnant woman couldn't have sex,
she felt pretty sure her obstetrician wouldn't approve.
He'd even said that any little thing could drive her

into premature labor. At any rate, she just couldn't see herself getting naked in front of Eli in her current condition. Much as she wanted to.

"Eli...we can't make love."

"Is that what's got you worried?"

"Why would you want to marry someone you can't have sex with?" she blurted out.

He surprised her by laughing. "I presume that's not a permanent condition. I mean, Thing One and Thing Two have to come out into the real world before too long."

"Yes, but then I'll still be fat, and we'll have bottles and diapers and...twins, you know."

"I recall you mentioned something about twins."

"Things won't be the same. Not like they were in Roan."

"Things never stay the same," he said. "At least, they don't for me. That's one lesson I've learned. But I don't see any reason in the world we can't have fulfilling—no, fantastic—sex after you recover from childbirth."

She sighed. "You're waiting for me to make a decision about getting married."

"No hurry."

"It'd be nice if the babies could be born in wedlock, I suppose. I know that's old-fashioned, but Jester is a small town."

"I'd prefer that, too."

"They'll hear wild stories about their origins as it is. That twit reporter from Pine Run, Harvey Brinkman, has already dubbed them 'Fortune's Twins.'"

"How did the newspaper find out you weren't having just one?"

Gwen shrugged. "Someone in town is feeding gossip to the media. First it was when baby Max was left on the counter at The Brimming Cup. Then it was Jack and Melinda getting engaged. Then Amanda adopting her half siblings, and Jennifer Faulkner coming to town to claim her inheritance and then marrying the sheriff. Then Sam and Ruby Cade's almost-divorce. It's become a regular soap opera around here since the lottery, and apparently the public continues to be interested in us.

"Needless to say news of my pregnancy didn't escape anyone's notice. Harvey called me a few days ago to confirm I was having twins. I didn't see any reason to deny it."

"I hope you're keeping these articles for the kids' scrapbooks."

"I never even thought of that." Maybe the articles would seem amusing after a while, but right now Gwen just wanted to forget about them.

Eli stood and helped her to her feet. "Come on, let's get some fresh air."

They left the theater, meeting several people arriving for the evening show. Finn Hollis smiled a greeting, his eyes filled with curiosity at seeing them out together.

Gwen wasn't quite ready to return to the boarding-house, so she ambled toward Jester Community Park across the street from her home. She'd always loved the park. It was huge, with a baseball diamond, a small pond, playground equipment and several shade trees. The grass was still green from summer. She headed for the swing set and claimed a swing.

He sat in the swing next to hers. "What happened there?" he asked, pointing to a huge bare spot on the lawn, where a foundation was still visible.

"That used to be our pavilion. It was so nice—wonderful in the summer for band concerts. It collapsed last March during our Founder's Day celebration."

"You have a festival in March? In Montana?"

"We are a hardy lot, us Montanans. We bundle up every March and brave the snow. In fact, we thought it was just too much snow on the roof that made the pavilion collapse. But Luke McNeil, our sheriff, investigated. He got Sam Cade to help. Sam was in the military and Luke thought Sam could use his covert operative skills to discover something.

"Luke suspected the pavilion was sabotaged, and then someone tried to burn it to destroy the evidence. A structural engineer confirmed Luke's suspicions."

"Do they know who did it?"

Gwen shook her head. "The investigation is ongoing, and everybody has theories, but no hard evidence." No one would dare voice their suspicions aloud, but a couple of obvious suspects came to mind—like Bobby Larson. One reason the town council had balked over building a hotel in the park was a reluctance to tear down the historic pavilion, which had been built in the 19th century.

Personally, Gwen had another suspect in mind.

Wyla Thorne was just mean enough—and bitter enough about losing out on the big jackpot—that she might do something like destroy a beloved landmark—just to spite the whole town.

"Whoever did it," Gwen said, "I don't think they meant for anyone to be injured. It was just bad luck Melinda Hartman was standing there when the pavilion fell. She wasn't hurt badly," Gwen hastened to add when she saw the look of concern on Eli's face.

Gwen scuffed her tennis shoe in the dirt, swaying her swing to and fro.

"Want me to push you?" Eli asked.

She hoped he was kidding. "You'd probably throw your back out."

He sat in the swing beside hers. "Don't do that. Don't denigrate yourself. I happen to think your current condition makes you beautiful."

"You're just saying that to butter me up."

"No, I'm not. I find you attractive. After all, you're carrying my daughters."

"Do you mind that they're both girls?"

"I'm thrilled they're girls. I plan to spoil them rotten."

Damn. He knew all the right things to say. "You're wearing me down, you know."

"I was hoping so. What's holding you back?"

She sighed again. "I think marriages should be based on love."

"And I think love is overrated. I'm not sure I believe in it."

"Oh, it's real, all right. Just talk to Shelly and Connor. Or…or Jack and Melinda or Dev and Amanda or Jennifer and—''

''Cupid's been busy in Jester.''

''Yeah. I guess he ran out of steam when it came to you and me.''

''Maybe it's not too late for us. Lots of couples fall in love after they're married.''

''But you don't believe in love.''

''If anyone could change my mind, it's you.''

Well, that was something, at least. Gwen basked in the small spotlight of hope he'd given her. That hope gave her the courage to forge ahead with the unpleasant matter she'd been avoiding. ''There is something else. Before I say yes—there's the matter of a prenuptial agreement.''

Eli laughed nervously. ''I'm glad you brought it up instead of me.''

''Then you're willing to talk about it?''

''Of course. My attorney is a real control freak. I don't really care, but he insists I protect my interests.''

Her heart sank. This was the reason she'd put off this confrontation for so long. ''I see.''

''My lawyer drew up some preliminary terms. I have them in my room. I'll show them to you, if you like.''

''You were pretty sure I'd cave in eventually, weren't you?''

''I was hoping. You'll probably want your own attorney to weigh in on the terms. I'm pretty open, just so my business is protected.''

But she didn't want his business! Her head was spinning. His mechanic shop wasn't the issue. Her million-plus dollars was. "I'll agree to protect your business," she said slowly, "so long as you return the favor."

"Why would I want your boarding—oh, you mean the money."

"Yes." *Duh.*

He looked amused. "I believe the agreement simply sets up safeguards to keep our property and finances separate. It protects both of us."

This seemed a bit too easy. "All right," she agreed hesitantly. "That sounds fine."

"So when's the wedding?"

"I'll have to think about it." This was the most emotionless marriage proposal she'd ever heard of. What if her children asked her someday about how their father had asked her to marry him? "This isn't how it's supposed to be!"

"And getting you pregnant with twins wasn't supposed to happen, either, but it did. There's not exactly time for a courtship and flowers and romantic walks in the moonlight."

"But those things are important to me."

She could see the frustration building behind his eyes. He was trying to be patient with her, she could tell.

"Oh, never mind," she grumbled. "It's my crazy hormones talking. You're absolutely right. I'm being impractical. If we're going to get married, we should get on with it.'' So much for the big church wedding she'd fantasized about since she was a girl.

''Is that a yes?''

''Yes, Eli, I'll marry you.''

Had she just said yes? Was she engaged? Had she just changed the course of her entire life?

## Chapter Six

Eli allowed himself a sigh of relief. He hadn't realized how important Gwen's answer was to him until she'd finally said yes.

"Well, that was harder than it should have been." He smiled, then took her into his arms and sealed the bargain with a kiss. The kiss was a bit more chaste than the one in the movie theater had been, but Eli didn't figure Gwen would appreciate being fondled in a public park.

He pulled back slightly and gazed into her eyes. "I have just one more question."

"Shoot."

"Do I have to wait 'til our wedding night before we sleep together?"

"Oh, Eli, I already told you—"

"I'm not talking about sex. I just want to hold you. Jeez, woman, I've missed you."

"How could you miss someone you only spent one night with?"

He couldn't explain it, but it was true. From the moment she'd walked out of that hotel room, he'd ached for her. He'd been devastated when he'd obliterated her phone number, and had thought of her a hundred times a day since then.

"You're not answering the question," he said. "Again."

"I'm embarrassed. I don't want you to see me... naked. Like this."

"I know you don't believe me, but I think you're more beautiful than ever. You're a madonna, you're every woman."

"Every fat woman."

"Gwen..."

"Okay, okay. No, I don't think we should start sleeping together until we're married. Grandmother would roll over in her grave if I shacked up with you under her roof."

"Then can we hurry up and get married?"

"Yes."

"Can I take you to a hotel before then? Surely your grandmother's ghost doesn't hang out at hotels, waiting for you to show up with a man you're not yet married to." All this talk of sleeping together and hotels and getting Gwen naked was getting Eli hot and bothered again, so he was relieved by what she said next.

"We can go into Pine Run tomorrow and get the license and the blood test and...and we'll just do it. *Before* that wretched Harvey Brinkman gets wind of it. I do not want to see my picture in the paper as 'Pregnant Millionaire Bride.'"

"Amen to that."

Eli walked Gwen back to the boardinghouse with mixed feelings. He knew marrying Gwen was the right thing to do. His sense of honor wouldn't allow him to settle for any other solution, and he looked forward to having a permanent home. But certainly his proposal hadn't been met with the enthusiasm he'd hoped for. With all the discussion about a prenup, it had sounded more like a corporate acquisition than a romantic exploration of the future.

Of course, he was the one who didn't believe in love. Or so he'd said. Maybe it wasn't so much that he didn't believe in the emotion, as that he wasn't sure it could lead to a happy future. Love was too wispy, too unpredictable. He figured he and Gwen had a better chance than some starry-eyed young couple all consumed with love, their reasoning blotted out by passion.

Not that he and Gwen didn't have passion. But at least they were planning rationally for the future.

GWEN WAS NERVOUS about her trip into Pine Run with Eli. She hadn't told anyone of her impending marriage, not even Sylvia. She was determined to keep her wedding ceremony private. The last thing she needed was photographers showing up. She didn't want any pictures to commemorate the event. Of course her daughters would know she'd been pregnant when she and Eli got married. That kind of gossip was hard to stifle. But she didn't want them to endure the embarrassment of seeing images of their mother hugely pregnant at her wedding.

Since she didn't know who was leaking information to the press, she didn't trust anyone with her secret. She would grab Sylvia at the last minute as her maid of honor, because Sylvia would never speak to her again if she didn't, but that was all.

Gwen dressed with care in her best maternity dress, a navy blue shirtwaist with tiny sprigs of ivy printed on the fabric. She pulled her long hair into a ponytail, rather than her customary bun, because she was tired of looking matronly and having people like Val Simms call her "Ms. Tanner."

Right after a breakfast of fruit and yogurt, Gwen met Eli in the small parking area beside her house. She'd intended to take her Mercedes to Pine Run, because she couldn't face another spin in the car she'd privately dubbed the "Bucket-o'-Bolts." But Eli was already there, warming up his classic Jaguar instead.

She supposed that was all right. She remembered his car passing her on the highway the day he'd come to town. She'd had no idea it was him, but she'd coveted his car.

"Ready?" Eli asked as he opened the passenger door for her.

She sank into the luxurious leather seat. "Ready." She clasped her hands in what was left of her lap to keep them from trembling.

They went to her lawyer's office first. He read Eli's draft of the pre-nup, which was straightforward and reflected exactly the terms they'd talked about. Her lawyer could find nothing to object to and gave it his seal of approval, so they signed the darn thing. She was glad to put that behind her.

The license came next, then the blood test. Gwen had insisted they not have blood drawn at the Jester Medical Center, or everybody would know what they were up to. Eli wasn't quite sure why all the secrecy was necessary, but he went along with her wishes. They went to All Saints Hospital for the test.

Finally, they sought out a justice of the peace to schedule the ceremony itself. They decided on the following Friday, less than a week away. Gwen figured the sooner the better, since Thing One and Thing Two, as Eli had christened them, had been kicking up a storm. She hoped she was wrong, but her newly discovered mother's intuition told her she wasn't going to make it to her due date in mid-October.

It was almost noon by the time they were finished with the errands. Though Gwen was tired, she had to admit the morning hadn't been the chore she'd anticipated. Eli had made each step of the process enjoyable. He'd even held her hand when the technician was drawing her blood, perhaps believing she might be squeamish. She didn't bother telling him that since her pregnancy, she'd had so much blood drawn that needles didn't bother her in the slightest.

Instead of heading home right away, Eli insisted they visit a charming downtown café for lunch. Gwen longed for a couple of greasy pork chops, but she made herself order a chicken caesar salad. She'd discovered recently that greasy foods didn't sit well with her. Besides, she didn't want her daughters to be born with clogged arteries.

Eli ordered a cheeseburger and fries, and made no apologies.

She was about to reach for a french fry off his plate when one of the babies treated her to a particularly violent kick. Something must have shown on her face, because Eli stared at her, concern clouding his gorgeous blue eyes. "Gwen, what's wrong?"

She smiled. "Nothing. It's just that one of your daughters is going to be the first female place kicker for the Seahawks."

"You mean the Broncos," he corrected her. Then the true meaning of her words dawned on him. "They're kicking?"

"One of them is, anyway."

A look of delight descended over his face. "Can I feel?"

"What? In here?"

He scooted over to her side of the booth. "There's nothing wrong with a man wanting to feel his babies kick. Anyway, the tablecloth hides you." He placed his hand gingerly on her abdomen.

Resigned to the fact he was going to do this, she slid his hand to the place where the tiny foot—or maybe it was an elbow—had been poking out moments before.

"They've been kicking me since five months," she said. "I used to think it was special, too." Now, her usual reaction was to hope neither of them kicked her in the bladder.

"It is special," he said just as another kick came. He smiled like he'd found gold. "There it is. How often does it happen?"

"Gosh, all the time, now." But looking at the expression of awe on Eli's face, she couldn't help but reclaim some of the magic she'd discovered early in her pregnancy, before she'd gotten so tired and anxious. "Here, there's another one on this side." She moved his hand over. She'd be happy to let the babies kick all day if she could continue to watch Eli's face. She was sure she'd never seen him so unguarded with such an uncomplicated emotion.

A sense of rightness stole over her. Maybe she'd misjudged Eli. Maybe he was motivated by nothing more than a sincere desire to do the right thing, for her and the twins. And maybe, just maybe, they would fall in love. Sometimes she thought she might be halfway there, though she often reminded herself she didn't know the man well enough to love him.

They held hands as they walked down the sidewalk toward Eli's car, which Gwen found sweetly endearing. But before they reached the car, Eli pulled her into a little shop. It took her a moment to realize they were in a jewelry shop.

He grinned at her. "We have to have rings."

She hadn't even thought of that. She wasn't much of a jewelry person except for the gold locket that had belonged to her grandmother, which she wore on special occasions. "All right. We could buy some tasteful, matching gold bands."

"Not on your life. You're going to get a boulder to wear on your hand."

"That's not very practical," she objected. "It'll just get in the way."

"A wedding ring should not be practical," he insisted as he inspected the contents of a glass case. Obviously seeing nothing he liked, he moved onto another case, then another.

Finally, in a case of estate jewelry, something caught his eye. "May I see the one behind the pink tourmaline?" he asked the clerk. "Yes, that's the one. And the canary diamond. And…the square-cut diamond with the baguettes."

It sounded to Gwen as if Eli knew his jewelry. Where had a mechanic learned such things? It again occurred to her that she knew very little about her husband-to-be. Had he been married before and learned about rings when he was shopping for his first bride? His first three brides?

*Oh, stop it!* She was becoming paranoid.

"Gwen, come try these on," Eli called to her.

He didn't have to ask twice. The rings he'd chosen were breathtaking. Of course, they looked even more sensational when showcased against her less-than-elegant hands, with their calluses and short, practical nails.

She tried on all three, dutifully admiring each. She caught sight of the price tag on one ring. It was over four thousand dollars.

"I'm not sure any of these suit me," she said diplomatically. She couldn't possibly condone spending that kind of money on a frivolous ring. Especially one she might not be able to wear in a few months, if they couldn't get their marriage to work. She was just too practical, influenced by her Depression-raised grandmother.

"Are there any in here you like?" he said.

She looked around, finally spotting a thin gold band with a row of three diamond chips. It was on sale for seventy-nine dollars. "How about that one?"

Eli frowned. "You'll make me look like a piker."

"Oh, I see. We're out to impress our friends."

"They're your friends. And I need all the help I can get convincing them I'm doing right by you."

She sighed. Perhaps a compromise was in order. But she didn't want to seem as if she were competing with Amanda's ring. Dev Devlin had bought her a four-karat diamond. But then, Amanda could wear such a ring and pull it off. She had a style and flair Gwen felt she lacked.

She hunted around in the cases some more. "That one?" She pointed to a half-karat solitaire.

Eli shook his head.

She found one a bit larger, with two small diamonds on either side. "That one?"

"I'd like you to wear a ring people don't need a magnifying glass to see. Something that will have a chance against your radiance."

"Oh, now you're piling it on." Radiance? Her?

They finally settled on a two-karat oval flanked by six smaller stones. It still seemed huge to Gwen, but at least the setting was flat and wouldn't get caught on everything.

Gwen wandered to another part of the store while Eli paid for the ring with his credit card. She wondered if she would be liable for his debts after they were married. She pictured hordes of bill collectors standing on her porch with their hands out, and Eli long gone.

Her mother had been forced to deal with just such a scenario, all while fighting a post-partum infection. She'd ultimately lost that fight, dying long before Gwen was old enough to remember her. Her paternal grandmother had told her that her mother, faced with the shambles her life had become after Willie Tanner left her, had simply lost the will to live.

Gwen would never act like that, she vowed. Even if Eli turned out to be another Willie Tanner, she would press on for the sake of her babies. They would not grow up without a memory of either parent, as she had.

Though the temptation was strong to buy Eli his own gaudy ring—one with a huge horseshoe of diamonds, for instance—she instead bought him a plain gold band. He seemed pleased by her choice.

Eli's ring had to be sized, but Gwen's fit perfectly, so they took it with them. Eli made Gwen put it on before he even started the car. "It's a sexist custom, making a bride wear an engagement ring so everybody knows she's taken. Like the groom can't trust her otherwise," Gwen said.

"It's not you I don't trust. It's all those other men."

"Oh, yes. That long line of men at my door. No worries, Eli. These days, men practically cross the street to avoid me."

Still, she put the ring on and thoroughly enjoyed it. It was gorgeous, something she would never have bought for herself. Sylvia would be green with envy—and probably would go buy herself an even bigger diamond.

Gwen relaxed during the drive home. She'd really enjoyed herself today, for the first time in weeks. Her sense of peace and well-being lasted exactly as long as it took to drive back to Jester, where Stella met her on the front porch, an anxious look on her face.

"Stella, whatever's wrong?"

"Nothing. It's just…you *are* going to invite me, aren't you?"

"Pardon me?"

"To the wedding!"

Gwen glared suspiciously at Eli. "You told!"

He shrugged helplessly. "I never said a word."

"Oh, honey, no one had to tell me. It was written all over your face this morning. I knew something was up when you and Eli disappeared mysteriously right after breakfast, you all dressed up. I made a lucky guess. And even if I hadn't guessed, you're wearing an engagement ring!" Stella grabbed Gwen's hand to get a closer look.

"You haven't told anyone, have you?" Gwen asked worriedly.

"Why would you want to keep it a secret?"

"I don't want that Harvey Brinkman to show up."

Stella wrinkled her pert nose. "That fellow is pretty unpleasant. I see your point."

"I'll let you come to the wedding if you promise not to breathe a word to anybody."

"Not even Irene and Oggie?"

Gwen realized she was being unreasonable. All three of her boarders were like family. And she could hardly wait to see the look on Oggie's face when he heard the news. He would probably think all that scowling had finally served its purpose.

"All right, you can tell Irene and Oggie. But tell them to keep it quiet. We're sort of eloping, after all, and you can't have a proper elopement if everybody in town knows!"

Eli just chuckled and headed for his room to change into his work clothes.

Stella beamed like a lighthouse. "Oh, honey, I'm so happy for you. I just knew you two could work things out. What a lovely family you'll make."

It was on the tip of Gwen's tongue to say they hadn't worked much of anything out, except what their matrimonial status would be. Where would they live? What if Eli wanted to up and move back to Denver? He'd *said* he would never interfere with her custody, but if they were married, his rights would automatically be equal to hers.

"Gwen, dear, you have a strange look on your face."

"Just borrowing trouble," Gwen said, shaking her

head. But her distrust of men, and Eli in particular, just refused to be squelched.

"It's only natural for you to worry about the future at this stage in your life. But everything will work out well for you. I feel it in my bones, and my bones never lie."

If only Gwen could trust Stella's bones!

GWEN KNEW something was up. Irene, Stella and Oggie all acted nervous during their dinner of baked chicken, string beans and mashed potatoes, and they said absolutely nothing about her upcoming marriage. But as soon as Irene had cleared the plates, Stella disappeared, returning a short time later with a cake topped with candles.

"Happy engagement!" her three friends said together. Eli looked embarrassed, but Gwen was touched. The cake, obviously homemade, sagged a bit on one side.

"Did you make the cake, Stella?" she asked innocently after she and Eli blew out the candles together.

"How did you know?"

"Just a guess." But if she hadn't known before she tasted the cake, she'd have known after. She hadn't tasted anything that chalky since the last time her grandmother gave her milk of magnesia. But she gamely managed to choke down most of a small slice. Eli looked as if he were having similar trouble.

"Yoo-hoo, anyone home?"

Gwen cringed. It was Wyla Thorne. Because she

was Stella's friend, she thought she had the perfect right to barge right into the boardinghouse any time of the day or night without knocking.

"We're in the dining room, Wyla," Stella called to her. "Come on in."

Wyla appeared in the doorway, her thin body encased in skintight pink polyester pants and a matching pink-and-white striped sweater that clashed with her frizzy red hair.

"I didn't mean to interrupt dinner," she said. "Oh, my, whose birthday is it?"

Everyone at the table looked around uneasily. No one wanted to tell her, since Gwen had told them she wanted the engagement kept a secret. But no one wanted to lie, either. Since Gwen was the one who'd put them all in the uncomfortable position, she spoke up.

"It's not a birthday. We're celebrating Eli's and my engagement."

"Well, it's about time!" Wyla gave Gwen a dutiful hug. "If you need any advice about the wedding, just call. I'm something of an expert, you know."

"You're a wedding planner?" Eli asked politely.

"Oh, no, honey. I've been married twice. And divorced, still looking for Lucky Husband Number Three. Of course, I'm beginning to think that's never going to happen. Every time a good-looking man comes to town, one of the hot young things nabs him." She gave Eli a meaningful up and down. "So, when's the date?"

"It's next Friday," Eli said, apparently not noticing Gwen's toe thwacking against his shin.

"Am I invited?"

"It's just immediate family," Gwen said.

"But you don't have any family left," Wyla pointed out. She had the tact of an anvil falling from a twenty-story building.

"We're her family," Irene said quietly but firmly. "Gwen and Eli want a small, private ceremony. I hope you'll respect their privacy."

"Oh, of *course!*" Wyla said. "At this late date, I don't blame you a bit, Gwen."

Eli pressed his lips together so tightly they turned white. Gwen almost wished he wouldn't hold back. She was too polite to lash out at Wyla, but she didn't mind it when someone else did. The woman was unbearably rude, and she'd only gotten worse since the lottery win. She seemed to blame the whole town for her unfortunate choice not to throw her dollar in that week.

Even Stella seemed a bit taken aback by Wyla's rudeness. But Stella was the last person to take anyone to task. She always made allowances for Wyla, citing her unfortunate childhood and her trampy mother.

"We better go," Stella said. "We'll be late for the movie."

"I thought we'd skip the movies tonight and go to that dance club in Roan," Wyla said. "What's it called, Gwen?"

"The Wild Mustang," Gwen said between her gritted teeth.

"That's it. I hear it's a great place to meet studly men."

Stella scooted her chair out so quickly she almost knocked it over. "All right. Let me get my purse."

Oggie spoke up for the first time. "Stella, I'm not sure you should go to a place called The Wild Mustang. Sounds dangerous."

Wyla just laughed.

Poor Oggie. He was so smitten, it hurt to watch him.

"Why don't you go with them?" Gwen suggested.

"Gwen! I'm the vice principal. I can't hang out in bars. What kind of example would I be setting?"

"One hopes none of your students would see you there. Anyway, it's a very nice club." Except on Wet T-Shirt Night, but that's on Tuesdays. "You'd have fun."

"We'd love to have you," Wyla said with uncharacteristic generosity. "You can protect us from all those men stampeding to get to us."

"I'm sure you can take care of yourself," Oggie murmured, embarrassed.

Stella and Wyla left, much to everyone's relief.

"I'd like to just pinch her head off sometimes," Irene said. "And now that *she* knows about your wedding, it'll be all over town by noon tomorrow. Mark my words."

## Chapter Seven

Irene was right.

Gwen spent her morning doing what she'd done almost every day since coming home from the hospital—she sat on the porch, wrapped in an afghan and reading. It was just about eleven when her first visitor arrived, Amanda Devlin. Gwen stood up to greet her friend.

"I just wanted to drop off this book Irene ordered," Amanda said with a studied, casual air. "I know she's been anxious to read it." Amanda's gaze darted to Gwen's left hand, and she smiled slightly.

"Yes, Eli and I are getting married," Gwen blurted out, "and yes, that's a new ring. Would you like to see it?"

Amanda's smile grew and she threw her arms around Gwen. "Oh, I'm so happy for you. When Eli showed up here, I just knew it would all turn out okay."

Gwen sank back into her rocking chair. "Does everyone know?"

Amanda nodded. "I'm afraid you and Eli have

been the main topic of conversation at the bookstore this morning. Wyla told everybody, but I was sent over to get the straight scoop from you since we can't trust Wyla to get the details right. Why do you look so sad?''

"We were trying to keep news of the wedding quiet. I have so much to worry about already, and I didn't want any reporters taking pictures. I mean, would you want wedding pictures where you look like you're carrying a watermelon under your dress?''

Amanda laughed. "Oh, poor Gwen. I get your drift. But I'm afraid you're fighting a losing battle. Harvey Brinkman is getting his information from somebody in this town.''

"Probably Bobby Larson," Gwen grumbled. "He positively crows every time an article appears in the paper about Jester. And he tried to change the name of our town to 'Millionaire.'''

"Thank goodness the town council voted him down." She paused, hesitating.

"What?" Gwen asked.

"Is it okay to ask when the wedding is?''

"Friday, 10:00 a.m. But we're just going to the justice of the peace. It's not a big deal.''

"I guess that means I'm not invited.''

Gwen crumbled at the hurt look in Amanda's eyes. "If you really want to come, you can. But there won't be much to see. And don't tell anyone else I invited you.''

"What about Sylvia? She'll be there, won't she?''

Gwen gasped. "Sylvia! Oh, my gosh, I better tell

her. She'll be really mad at me if she hears it through the grape—'' Gwen cut herself off. It was too late. Sylvia was marching down Main Street toward Gwen's house, her short blond hair whipping around in the brisk wind. She hadn't even bothered to remove her purple apron. ''Uh-oh, I'm in trouble.''

''I'd love to witness this, but I have to get back to the shop,'' Amanda said with a wink. ''I'll do what I can as far as damage control—about the gossip, I mean.''

''Thanks.''

Sylvia didn't even acknowledge Amanda as the two women passed each other on the steps. She stormed up to the porch, intent on confronting Gwen. ''How could you? How could you keep your wedding a secret from your best friend? I kept your secret all this time. I never told one single person how you ended up pregnant, though Lord knows everyone was pumping me for information.''

''I was going to tell you. In fact, I want you to be my maid of honor.''

''You do?'' All the fire went out of Sylvia. ''I'd love to. But how can I be your maid of honor if I don't know when the wedding is?''

''It's Friday morning.''

Sylvia clapped her hands together. ''I'm so happy for you!''

It seemed everybody was happy for Gwen, except Gwen herself.

Sylvia immediately sensed Gwen's mood. She

pulled up a chair next to Gwen's. "What is it, sweetie?"

Gwen couldn't help it. Her eyes filled with tears. "I just always envisioned my wedding as a bit more romantic than this. Remember when we were in high school, and we used to pick out our colors and flowers, design our dresses, choose our bridesmaids?"

"Let's see, you wanted a winter wedding, a white velvet dress, forest-green bridesmaid dresses and red and white roses."

"And you wanted a summer wedding in a garden, with an ecru organdy dress, peach bridesmaid dresses and…oh, yeah, a crown of daisies."

Sylvia wrinkled her nose at the memory. "We had everything settled except the identity of the groom. At least you've solved that problem."

"Real life is a lot different from girlhood fantasy, though."

"Oh, come on, Gwen. He's not everything you've ever dreamed of? He's Prince Charming in blue jeans."

"I don't know anything about him! He's kind, he's handy around the house, he likes cars and bad sci-fi movies…and Irene's dog. I caught him sneaking a bone to Benny this morning."

"Well, there you have it." Sylvia grinned.

"I only found out yesterday how old he is, when we filled out paperwork."

"How old is he?" Sylvia immediately wanted to know.

"Thirty-five."

"So what else do you need to know?"

"His family. Where he grew up, where he went to school. How he ended up as a mechanic. How he learned carpentry. He knows intimate details of my pregnancy, and I don't know his shoe size."

"Why don't you just ask him?"

That was a good question. "I feel nosy asking."

Sylvia knocked lightly on Gwen's head with her knuckles. "Hello, wake up, Gwendolyn. Men *like* women to ask them about themselves. Once you get him started, you'll probably never shut him up. They love to expound on their favorite subject—themselves."

"Not Eli. He doesn't open up, and I'm not good at coaxing information out of him."

Sylvia squeezed Gwen's hand. "Maybe it's better this way. A little mystery never hurt a relationship." She checked her watch. "Oh, shoot. I left Regina Larson's hair up in perm rods. She's going to have an afro if I don't get back soon."

"What's your rush?" Gwen said, imagining the mayor's wife looking like Bozo the Clown.

"Don't be mean, Gwen, it's not becoming." With a parting promise that she would style Gwen's hair for the wedding, Sylvia turned and trotted down the steps.

She had hardly cleared the porch before Bobby Larson's gold Cadillac pulled up to the curb in front of Gwen's house. Gwen really wasn't up to more verbal sparring with the mayor, and she considered darting inside and pretending to be indisposed. But he'd already seen her, she realized. He was waving as he made his way up the walkway to her porch.

"Hello, there, Gwen," he said with an unctuous smile. "How are you feeling these days?"

"Fine, just fine," she replied, unwilling to share her aches and pains with him. "And yourself?"

"Well, I'm a little concerned, actually." Without invitation he settled into the chair Sylvia had sat in a few minutes ago.

Gwen groaned silently. The mayor sure had spent a lot of time *concerned* about her lately.

"I understand you've decided to marry this Garrett character."

"Yes, I have. And I'm sorry you and Eli got off on the wrong foot. He's a very decent man."

"Is that so? Well, I'll have you know I've done some checking into your Eli's background. He's not the paragon you think he is."

"You really shouldn't have done that," Gwen said, her anger rising. "That's an invasion of Eli's privacy!"

"Then you don't want to know what I found out?"

"If there's anything I need to know about Eli's past, I'm sure he'll tell me."

Bobby just sat there, looking out toward the park—visualizing his precious hotel, no doubt. Now that the gazebo was out of the way, the town council had actually been considering Bobby's proposal. He was convinced the added tax revenue and the jobs and the boost to tourism would more than make up for the loss of some public park property.

Gwen hated herself for what she said next, but she couldn't help herself. "All right, just tell me. What did you find out about Eli that's so terrible?" *And please don't let it be that he has three wives, ten children and a prison record.*

"He filed for bankruptcy a few years ago."

Though it was a warm day, Gwen felt an Arctic chill wiggling up her spine. Not that bankruptcy was the same as a criminal record. But it gave Gwen pause. She remembered how easily Eli whipped out his credit card to pay for her ring.

"I can see by your face he didn't tell you that," Bobby said.

"I didn't ask him for a personal financial statement," she countered.

"Well, here's something else he probably didn't tell you. He wasn't born with the name Eli Garrett. He changed it at some point. Filed for a new birth certificate and everything."

Gwen swallowed the lump in her throat. That little piece of news was a bit more ominous. "How did you find this out?"

"Oh, I have my sources," Bobby said. "I've always thought of you as a daughter, Gwen, especially since you don't have any family of your own now. I consider it my duty to look after your interests. And I'm not sure your interests are being served by marrying this character."

"Thank you for your concern," she said, though she didn't for one minute think Bobby's motives were altruistic. He was hoping to get her to give Eli his walking papers so Eli would leave town, clearing the way for Bobby to buy the house next door and Mac's Auto Repair. He would probably build his hotel in an L-shape around her house, just to spite her.

*Daughter, my foot.*

"I'll think about what you've told me," Gwen said, just to get rid of him.

It occurred to Gwen, after Bobby left, that he might be lying. But Bobby didn't usually lie outright unless he was pretty sure he could get away with it. If he'd made up this stuff about Eli, he would get caught.

She did intend to find out the truth of the matter. She would find out from Eli. When next she saw him, she would just ask him point-blank about his finances. If she was marrying him, she needed to know.

GWEN'S RESOLVE weakened when she saw Eli at lunch. The midday meal was the only one the boardinghouse didn't routinely provide, but her boarders were welcome to use the kitchen and prepare their own food. This day, Irene and Stella had gone to The Brimming Cup for lunch. Gwen, her stomach roiling over what Bobby Larson had told her, was determined for the babies' sake to eat something, so she'd settled on heating up some leftover chicken soup.

Eli entered the kitchen just as she'd turned on the burner. He wore a pair of overalls over a snug black T-shirt. She'd never thought of overalls as sexy before; but then, she'd never seen a pair filled out quite like Eli filled his. He had plaster dust in his hair and a smudge on his chin. She felt a ridiculous urge to wipe off the smudge herself—maybe with her tongue.

He smiled as he caught sight of her. "Hi, gorgeous." He set a paper sack on the counter and went to the sink to wash up. "I brought an extra sandwich from the coffee shop. It's yours if you want it."

"I'm having soup, thanks." She watched, fascinated, as he soaped up his strong hands and well-muscled forearms at her sink, then stuck his whole head under the faucet. Wordlessly she handed him a clean dishcloth.

"I guess I should have asked before I practically took a shower in your kitchen," he said sheepishly. "I just saw you looking all cool and composed, and suddenly I felt grimy."

"Listen, I don't complain when Irene gives Benny a bath in here, so I could hardly complain about you. Do you want something to drink?"

"Don't suppose you have a cold beer lurking in the fridge, do you?"

"I don't allow alcohol in the house." That had been her grandmother's policy. Her grandmother had felt so strongly about alcohol that Gwen had always wondered if her husband had been a drinker. Gwen was pretty sure her father had been. Drinking and gambling seemed to go together.

Gwen had continued the policy because no one had ever objected to it, and it seemed prudent, though she was not opposed to moderate social drinking.

Did Eli drink? It was pretty early in the day to be asking for beer.

"I'll settle for a soft drink, then."

She got him a Coke and a glass of ice, and a ginger ale for herself, while he unwrapped one of his sandwiches and put it on a plate. Then he got out a bowl and spoon for her, and a couple of paper towels for their napkins.

They worked pretty well together, she mused.

As they sat down to their meal, she tried to figure out how to broach the subject of finances. But she just couldn't make herself come out and ask him. So she went in the back door.

"You know, Eli, it occurs to me we don't know each other very well to be getting married."

"No, we don't," he agreed. "But how much can we learn in a couple of weeks?"

"I was just wondering if there was anything about your past that I ought to know."

"You mean, do I have any other children? Or perhaps a crazy wife locked up in an attic somewhere?"

He was teasing, wasn't he? But he didn't smile.

"I thought it wouldn't hurt to ask. I know this marriage probably wouldn't have been your choice were it not for the babies."

"Nor yours."

"But we are going to try to make it work, right? I mean, we're not getting married strictly to give the babies legitimacy, right? We're planning to stay married?"

"If at all possible, yes."

"Then I want to start this marriage on sound footing. No secrets between us."

"Gwen, what are you getting at? I don't have any other wives, present or former. No children. No prison record. I've never been committed to a mental institution. I've never filed for unemployment, and I'm up to date on my taxes. I'm in perfect health. Anything else?"

"Please, Eli, don't be insulted," Gwen said. "I'd just like to know you better, and I'd think you'd want to do the same with me. Are there any questions you'd like to ask me?"

He took a sip of his drink, seeming to ponder the question. Finally he asked, "Do you trust me?"

She hesitated just a fraction of a second before answering. "Yes."

But Eli didn't miss that flicker of uncertainty. She could tell by the way his jaw tensed and his hand clamped around his sandwich, squeezing so hard that mustard oozed out from the side.

"My instincts tell me you are an honorable and trustworthy person," she elaborated. "But my rational side wants reassurance, that's all. I'd like to know more about the man I'm going to be sleeping beside for the next fifty or sixty years."

He held out both hands in a gesture of surrender. "What you see is what you get. I'm a simple man with simple tastes."

"Who drives a 1960 Jaguar."

"Okay, simple tastes when it comes to everything but cars. I like working with my hands, I keep to myself—a little too much, maybe—and I'm kind to old ladies and small dogs. I will be a faithful husband and I'll try to set a good example for our children.''

He obviously wasn't going to volunteer the information she wanted. But if she came out and asked him, he would think she'd been snooping, and whatever trust he had in her would be shattered.

Eli's mouth firmed into a thin, tense line. ''You're not satisfied, are you. You want to know all the ugly details.''

''If you want to keep the details of your painful romantic relationships a secret, that's your choice. But I want to know about anything that might affect our marriage or our children. I think that's a fair request.''

''My past is a painful subject, and something I don't want to talk about. I can promise you nothing in my youth will rear its ugly head to threaten either you or our children. I've shut the door on those years—permanently.''

And that was all he was going to say on the subject, apparently.

''All right, then,'' she said gently. ''We won't speak of it again. But I'm a pretty open-minded and forgiving person. So if you ever want to talk about something—anything at all—you don't have to worry that I'll walk out on you. I'm marrying you for better or worse, and that includes mistakes from the past. It's the future that really matters to me.''

''Thank you, Gwen,'' he said, and she felt he really meant it. ''I do have a question for you.''

''Shoot.''

''Have you given any thought to names?''

"For the babies? I thought we'd settled on Thing One and Thing Two."

"Seriously. I want names picked out before they're born."

He sounded pretty intense about this, so she applied some brain cells to the question. "My grandmother's name was Abigail. I've always liked that name, and I would love to honor her by naming a child after her...."

"But?"

"If there was only one baby, I wouldn't hesitate. But I couldn't honor one twin with that name and not the other."

"Do you have another grandmother?"

Gwen wrinkled her nose. "I'm not that close to her. Anyway, her name is Irma."

"Oh."

"Do you have any relatives you'd like to honor with a namesake?" she asked.

"No."

"No one? No sisters, grannies, a special aunt?"

"No."

Gwen took a deep breath. He hadn't even had to think about it. It saddened her to realize he'd grown up without a single female influence he considered worthy of honor. "I don't suppose you'd care to elaborate?" she asked.

He smiled stiffly. "It's the future that matters, remember?" He took a sip of his drink. "Why don't we name the twins after you? One can have your first name, the other your middle name."

Gwen frowned. "No way. I've never liked my first name. It's too old-fashioned. And my middle name is Rhymann."

"You mean, like the mustard?"

"Exactly like the mustard. Rhymann was my mother's maiden name. Her grandfather started the mustard company."

"Really. I love that stuff. 'The Mellow Mustard with a Kick.' So you're a mustard heiress?"

"Not anymore." She didn't elaborate. "Anyway, I think I want my daughters to have original names, so they don't have to live up to the memory of some ancestor. Names that go together, but are still distinct from each other."

"Like Mindy and Cindy?"

"Oh, Eli. Please."

"Too cutesy, huh?"

They tossed out dozens of names, then rejected them all. By the time they went to bed, they were no closer to naming the twins than when they'd started. She wondered if they were up to handling the real challenges of marriage if they couldn't work together to accomplish this simplest of tasks.

## Chapter Eight

The morning of Gwen and Eli's wedding dawned cold and overcast, with a few snow flurries. "It's too early for snow," Gwen grumbled as she dragged herself out of bed. But a small thrill of anticipation wiggled up her spine. Today was her wedding day. By ten-thirty, Eli would be her husband.

She could do a lot worse, she acknowledged. But she wished he weren't such a mystery to her. She'd always dreamed of having a husband who would be a partner in life with her, someone with whom she could share her most intimate secrets, a man who would stick with her through thick and thin.

Eli might eventually become that man. He hadn't run the other direction when she'd been ill, didn't seem to be repulsed by her ever-thickening middle. He seemed open to *her* sharing with him. But so far, it hadn't been a two-way street.

He'd been a little distant since their discussion in the kitchen a couple of days earlier, but she supposed that was to be expected. She'd hurt his feelings by questioning his honesty. Sylvia had been right—she knew all the important things about Eli. He was doing the honorable thing by marrying her. He'd been eager to sign the pre-nup, so her fortune was secure. If he had a few skeletons in his closet—well, who didn't? He was entitled to keep them private.

After all, though she'd been far more forthcoming about her life than he had, she hadn't told him every little thing. He knew she'd been a shy little girl with only a couple of close friends, and that she hadn't dated many boys, or later, men. But she hadn't told him how painfully shy she'd really been, or that she escaped reality through books and movies. And she hadn't admitted to the secret, lurid affair she'd had with that drifter when she was nineteen. Not even Sylvia knew about that.

He knew she'd been raised by her grandmother, and that both her parents had died when she was young. But she'd never admitted the terrible thing Willie Tanner—she refused to refer to him as her father—had done to her mother, using and abusing her and then discarding her like a used paper cup. She hadn't admitted to the shame and humiliation she'd felt when she'd learned that her birth father had virtually killed her mother.

But those were tender emotions that she would reveal to him in time, as their intimacy grew. And she believed he eventually would open up to her, too, once his trust in her had grown. For now, they knew the basics about each other, and that would have to be good enough.

Gwen pulled on a pair of wool maternity pants and

a huge sweater. She had a date with Sylvia to do her hair.

Only Stella, Irene and Oggie were at the table when Gwen came downstairs. Oggie was eating his customary poached egg on toast, but Stella and Irene were waiting for her. Gwen was dismayed at how quickly she'd grown accustomed to sleeping late.

"Where's Eli?" she asked, trying to hide her anxiety.

"He scooted out of here early," Stella said. "He claimed he had a few errands to run this morning."

She immediately started worrying that he wouldn't show up for the wedding.

"Now, Gwen, dear, don't fret. I don't think he has cold feet. Although he did seem a little nervous."

"What man wouldn't be nervous on his wedding day?" Oggie said. "Don't you ladies go putting worries into Gwen's head."

"Besides," Stella said, "he's not supposed to see you today until the wedding. It's bad luck. Sit down, dear. Breakfast is ready. Scrambled eggs and toast are warming in the oven."

"Is it your day to cook, Stella?" Gwen asked innocently as she took her chair at the head of the table. Irene and Stella had been alternating days, though not in a consistent pattern.

Stella nodded, and Gwen's heart sank. That meant runny eggs and burned toast. Her fears were confirmed when Stella set the plate in front of her. She took a few polite bites, then claimed she was too nervous to eat more. She would grab a muffin from

The Brimming Cup on her way to The Crowning Glory.

"Bundle up before you go outside," Irene cautioned. "It's not terribly cold, but there's a fierce north wind blowing."

Bundling up was something of a problem. Gwen couldn't button her coat over her stomach. Well, she only had to walk a block, she reasoned as she grabbed her purse and slipped out.

Sylvia was ready when Gwen arrived munching on a poppyseed muffin. "You baked muffins and you didn't bring me one?" she asked.

"I didn't bake anything. This is from The Brimming Cup. But as a matter of fact, I did bring you one." She pulled a rather flattened muffin from her purse.

"You do still love me!" Sylvia took the plastic-wrapped muffin and set it at her station. The two of them were alone in the salon, which had Sylvia's outrageous personal style stamped all over it. She'd used some of her lottery winnings to redecorate in shades of purple. She'd put in the most modern sinks, the fanciest chairs, the most high-tech lights. Everything matched, down to the purple hair dryers. The salon was so chic, in fact, that Sylvia had several customers who drove all the way from Pine Run to get their locks shorn at The Crowning Glory.

"I really love this place," Gwen said as she leaned back in the chair and fitted her neck into the sink's notch. "There's nothing more relaxing than having someone shampoo your hair. I want the works—conditioning, hot oil treatment, whatever you've got.''

"Your hair has gotten kind of strange since the pregnancy,'' Sylvia said as she adjusted the water temperature. "The texture is different. It's not unhealthy, just...different.''

"It's not as wavy as it used to be,'' Gwen agreed. "Kind of flat, especially the new part that's just grown out.''

"I could give you a perm.''

"No, no, no, not on my wedding day. That's inviting disaster. I'm sure you can style it so it looks good.''

"Of course I can. Your hair is beautiful, no matter what you do to it.''

Gwen relaxed and let Sylvia work her magic. When she was done, the image in the mirror shocked her. She looked elegant...no, better than that.

"I never said I wanted flowers woven into my hair,'' Gwen said, though she couldn't help smiling. "That was your fantasy, remember?''

"What would you have preferred, a snood?''

Gwen laughed. "That was my fantasy freshman year, after watching *The Lion in Winter*.''

"I can get rid of the flowers.''

"No, that's all right. I like them. But I have to run an errand at The Mercantile, and I'm going to feel silly.''

"What are you doing there?''

"I'm picking up Eli's wedding present.''

"Which is...''

"A key chain."

Sylvia grimaced and spun Gwen's chair around to face her. "You are pathetic. That is the most lame excuse for a wedding gift I can think of."

"No, hear me out. This is a great idea. See, earlier in the week I kind of pressed Eli about his past, and he felt that meant I didn't trust him. So I got him this gorgeous eighteen-karat key chain in the shape of a jaguar."

"You mean like his car?"

"No, the cat. It's symbolic. Anyway, I'm planning to put a copy of all my keys onto the chain. It's to show him I trust him. Get it?"

Sylvia looked uncertain. "It still sounds lame. I mean, you're rich. You could buy him a real Jaguar if you wanted."

"The cat?"

"No, the car. A man can't have too many classic cars."

"But I don't think Eli is planning to buy me a gift," she said. "We haven't talked about it, and I don't want him to feel like he has to reciprocate. He already bought the ridiculous ring."

Sylvia sighed. "It's a romantic ring. And I guess the key chain thing isn't too bad. Maybe a little sappy. Hey, why don't you put an antique key on the ring? And when he asks what it goes to, you say, 'It's the key to my heart.'"

"Talk about sappy!" But the idea wasn't half-bad. Still, Gwen felt their relationship was far too new and fragile to bring sticky emotions into the brew just yet.

Eli had said they might grow to love each other…
someday. She didn't want to rush him.

Sylvia sprayed Gwen's hair to within an inch of its
life, then forced her to wear a dorky plastic rain bonnet to protect the hairdo from possible snow and rain.

"My grandmother used to wear one of these,"
Gwen said.

"Aw, quit your complaining," Sylvia said. "Unless you want to look like a bedraggled Pekingese,
you'll wear the bonnet."

Gwen threw the hood up on her coat and scurried
to The Mercantile, hoping to see no one she knew.

She should have known anonymity was impossible
in a town the size of Jester. Finn Hollis was right at
the door as she entered, and he opened it for her.

"Good morning, Gwen," he said, then whispered,
"Happy wedding day. I understand you're trying to
keep it kind of quiet."

She smiled at Finn, who had always been a special
friend. When she'd been a little girl, and he still
worked at the library, he used to talk endlessly with
her about books and provide her with a steady supply
of good ones.

"I'm afraid everybody knows by now, but thanks
for trying," she said.

Next she saw Vicky McNeil Perkins, who was
Luke's sister and Doc's wife, buying school clothes
for the kids. Her long, jet-black hair was a testament
to her Native American heritage, but the blue eyes
were an interesting counterpoint. She shared a strong
family resemblance to Luke.

"They grow so fast," Vicky said, examining a corduroy romper. "This is so cute, but my youngest is already too big for things like this."

"It's darling," said Gwen, wondering if there might be a second one lurking nearby. She bought everything in twos these days.

"Listen," said Vicky, "I know you don't *need* clothes for your babies, and you probably want matching outfits, anyway, but I've got scads of nice baby clothes."

"I'd be tickled to take anything you want to give me," Gwen said sincerely. She liked the idea of passing baby clothes from one family to another and sharing a history. Just because she had plenty of money didn't mean everything her kids wore had to be brand-new. "And I don't plan to always dress the girls alike. I want them to develop their own styles."

Vicky smiled. "I'll put together a few of the cutest outfits. You know, they wear these things a few times, then they outgrow them. I'd love to see them again. Oh, and, good luck with your wedding." They talked as Vicki expertly rifled through stacks of folded jeans, picking out the correct sizes. "Are you nervous?"

"A little," Gwen confessed as she sorted through a rack of maternity dresses.

She'd vowed she wouldn't buy any more maternity clothes—she'd already gone nuts at Pea in the Pod and bought a closetful. For today, she was planning to wear a plain, blue wool dress with white trim. It wasn't very bridelike, but she would have looked silly in white satin with ruffles, beads and rosettes.

When she saw the pale green velvet dress, she abruptly changed her mind. It was the most gorgeous thing she'd ever seen, with an empire waist, satin ribbon trim and a heart-shaped neckline that would perfectly showcase her grandmother's locket. The fabric shimmered with a life of its own as Gwen ran her hand under it. She pulled the hanger off the rack and held the dress in front of her, then checked her image in a mirror.

"Oh, Gwen, that is lovely," Vicky said with an awe-inspired expression on her face. "No matter how hard I tried, I could never look as elegant as you— even when you're eight months pregnant."

Well, that did it. She was buying the dress.

"You'll be a beautiful bride," Vicky said with a tear in her eye. "Take lots of pictures, huh?"

For the first time, Gwen second-guessed her decision not to allow pictures. She might not be a traditional-looking bride, but the upcoming ceremony would be an important part of what would hopefully be a long history for her and Eli and their daughters.

"Let me know if I can do anything," Vicky offered with a quick hug. Then she headed to the cash register with an armload of jeans and flannel shirts.

Gwen started to head for the register herself. Val Simms, who'd recently been promoted to manager at The Mercantile, had the special-order key chain behind the counter. But then Gwen found herself jumping behind an overalls-clad mannequin. Eli was at the front counter, paying for a purchase.

Pure nosiness prompted Gwen to watch and see

what he'd bought. Val rang up his purchase—a suit, tie, dress shirt and shoes.

For the wedding, she realized.

She hoped it wasn't a financial strain for him. She didn't know how much mechanics made, but Eli had just purchased a house and a lot of building materials for the renovation. Plus, moving had probably been expensive, and he'd probably lost a customer base by relocating. He didn't seem to be hurting for cash, but she kept thinking about that bankruptcy and his ever-ready credit cards.

He was using plastic to pay for this purchase, too.

Gwen ducked behind a display of hunting gear as Eli left the store. He didn't see her, thank goodness. The pregnancy hadn't scared him off, but the rain bonnet might.

She went to the do-it-yourself key machine to copy all the keys on her ring while Val rang up Vicky's purchases. Finn got in line behind Vicky with a few sundries. By the time the keys were finished, Gwen was the only customer in the store.

Val waved to her. "I see you hiding over there, Ms. Tanner. Coast is clear, Mr. Garrett's long gone."

"How does the key chain look?" Gwen asked breathlessly.

Val's big blue eyes sparkled. "It's prettier in real life than in the catalog." She bent behind the counter to retrieve a small box. "Oh, Max, no, you cannot play with—oh, well, I guess it won't hurt him." Val's son, Max, was over a year old now, walking and talking and cute as a button. He'd discovered a Scotch tape dispenser. "It used to be so easy to keep him with me at work, but now he's into everything. I wear myself out chasing after him. I don't know how you'll manage it with two."

"I don't either," Gwen said with a nervous laugh.

"Of course, you'll have Mr. Garrett to help. Does he work?"

It was a simple enough question, but Gwen didn't know how to answer it. It was humiliating that she didn't know how her future husband earned his living. "He's a mechanic," she finally said.

Seeking to turn the conversation, Gwen opened the box. "Oh, it's lovely." She closely examined the finely crafted gold jaguar. She quickly put the keys she'd just made onto the key chain, then enclosed it in the box. "Can you wrap it?"

"Of course. On the house, since it's your wedding day and all."

"And I'm buying this." She didn't have time to try the green dress on, but with its roomy proportions, she was pretty sure it would fit.

"I had you in mind when I ordered that," Val said. "I didn't want to push it on you, since it's not very practical and sort of expensive, but I'm glad you found it on your own. Is it…are you going to wear it for your wedding?"

"Do you think I should?"

"I think it's perfect," Val enthused. "Green is the color of spring, of new life. You'll be a bright spot of color on a gray day. Everyone who looks at you will smile—as long as you lose the rain bonnet."

Gwen pulled her coat hood over her head. "Sylvia made me wear it."

Val finished wrapping the small box and handed it to Gwen. "I'll put the dress on your account. Now go home so you can take off the rain bonnet. No offense, but I don't think you want Mr. Garrett to see you in that thing. He might change his mind about the wedding."

Val was only teasing, but Gwen suddenly felt old and frumpy next to pretty, slender, youthful Val. Old and frumpy at twenty-nine. She would stick by her earlier decision about wedding photos.

ELI WAS NERVOUS as he put on the blue suit he'd bought off the rack at The Mercantile. He hadn't re-alized until this morning that he'd brought no dressy clothes with him when he'd moved to Jester. He had a closetful of tailored suits in his Denver house, but he seldom wore them. It hadn't occurred to him that he might need to dress up.

He'd been surprised at the quality of clothing he'd found at the small town general store. The suit was a good label, and fortunately it had fit him without al-terations. He wanted to look nice for Gwen. He wanted her to be proud of him.

Ah, hell, who was he kidding? He wanted to look good so she would want to jump his bones, like she did the night they met. He had high hopes for their wedding night. He found it strange that he was so attracted to her despite—or perhaps because of—her condition.

He hadn't seen her yet this morning, but Irene and Stella had assured him she was upstairs getting ready.

When he was dressed and as ruthlessly handsome as he was going to get, he emerged from his room. His three fellow boarders waited for him in the living room. "We're riding with you to Pine Run," Stella announced. "To make sure you get to the judge on time and sober. Not that we think you'd do otherwise, but weddings tend to turn sensible, grown men into lunatics."

He wasn't going to argue with her. He was nervous about riding alone with Gwen, anyway, worried he would say or do something to change her mind about marrying him. She'd seemed a little put out with him when they'd talked a few days ago. But her lack of trust in him had hurt. For most of his life, people had been suspicious of him based on nothing but the fact that he was an orphan who grew up poor. So now it irked him when anyone—even his fiancée—wanted to know facts and figures about his past.

His plan all along had been to win Gwen over with his actions—not by justifying his past. His actions toward Gwen since coming to Jester had been nothing but honorable. The size of his bank account shouldn't even enter into the equation. He certainly didn't care about *her* money.

Everyone stood and put on their coats.

"Shouldn't we wait for Gwen?" he asked, amused by their eagerness.

"Oh, she's riding with Sylvia," Irene explained.

"Don't you know it's bad luck for the groom to see the bride before the ceremony?"

"No way am I driving away from here without her," he said flatly. "Traditions be damned." The two women looked scandalized as he mounted the stairs two at a time, intending to let his bride know there'd been a change of plans. If Gwen got cold feet, he wanted to be there to reason her out of them.

When he knocked on Gwen's door, Sylvia opened it a crack. "What is it, Eli?"

"I want to see Gwen."

"Well, you can't. But you can talk to her if you want." She called over her shoulder. "Gwen? Your very handsome groom wants to talk to you."

"What does he want?" she called back, sounding distressed.

"I want us to drive to our wedding together. Is that too much to ask?"

"Yes! Go with Irene and the others. I'll see you there."

"Are you sure?"

"I'm sure!" she wailed, and he thought she might be crying.

"Gwen? Are you okay?"

"She's fine," Sylvia assured him. "Bridal jitters. I will get her to the judge's chambers on time, I promise. Now go."

Eli had no choice but to accommodate Gwen's wishes, but he wasn't happy about it. His new life with Gwen seemed to be getting off on a shaky first foot.

"I LOOK LIKE a watermelon with legs!" Gwen exclaimed, her eyes filling with tears. "This dress looked so pretty on the hanger, but—forget it, I'm wearing the blue wool.''

"You are not," Sylvia argued. "That dress is beautiful. A pregnant stomach is a beautiful thing, even prettier draped in luscious green velvet. And don't you dare start crying again, or I'll have to do your eye makeup all over."

"I don't know why I'm wearing makeup," Gwen groused as she struggled to get her dress shoes onto her swollen feet. She supposed it didn't matter what she wore. She'd still look huge, even in the unobtrusive blue wool.

When she stood, she teetered on the heels. "I haven't worn heels this high since last year sometime. Maybe I should switch to the black shoes."

"No! We're going to be late if we don't leave right now."

"Oh, all right. Can you get my bag?" Eli had told her to pack an overnight case. Though she'd explained she couldn't do a honeymoon—doctor's orders, no traveling—she'd agreed to one night in a hotel.

Just thinking about the night to come filled her stomach with butterflies. One minute she was thinking, *What if he suddenly realizes how truly undesirable I am and rejects me?* The next minute she was thinking, *Oh, God, what if he* does *want me?*

Somehow Gwen made it down all those stairs without misstepping and landing on her head. The house was deserted.

"Hadn't you better lock the front door?" Sylvia asked as they exited the house.

"Oh, I suppose." Gwen turned the dead bolt, which was stiff with disuse. It was so seldom the house was empty, she only locked it once in a while.

The snow flurries had stopped, but the sky was still gray. "Do you think the weather is a bad omen?" Gwen asked as she climbed into Sylvia's silver Lexus.

"Don't be silly. And stop biting your nails," Sylvia scolded as she started the engine. "You'll ruin the polish."

Gwen sat on her hands. "Am I doing the right thing?"

"Of *course* you're doing the right thing. You are going to die when you see how gorgeous he is in a suit."

"Oh, yes, that's a prime qualification for a husband," Gwen scoffed. "Must look good in suit."

"It's important to me," Sylvia said. "If I ever get married—and that's a big if—my husband is going to be gorgeous."

"But I don't know any more about him than the last time we talked. He seemed insulted that I was asking questions about him. Like I'm not entitled to be curious about my own husband?" She hadn't told Sylvia—or anyone, for that matter—about the bankruptcy.

"If you find out something terrible, you can have the marriage annulled on fraud grounds," Sylvia said with a teasing smile.

"That is *so* comforting."

"C'mon, Gwen, lighten up. My grandparents were married after knowing each other one day. One day! And they're still going strong after fifty years."

"You always hear stories like that about people's grandparents. You never hear the bad stories, though, because when the groom murders the bride on their wedding night, there are no kids or grandkids to tell the story to."

"You really *are* in a snit. But I'm going to write it off as nerves. You'll be fine once the vows are over."

Gwen hoped Sylvia was right.

When they finally reached the J.P.'s office, Gwen was stunned. The place was packed! She'd expected a few guests—her boarders and Amanda—but what was the mayor's wife doing here? And Wyla Thorne, of all people? Finn and a bunch of the guys from the barbershop? This was so embarrassing!

"Ah, there she is, the radiant bride," Finn said.

Oggie stepped forward to gallantly help her off with her coat. "Since your father's not here, I thought you might like me to give you away. But it's just an idea."

"Oh, Oggie, of course, I'd love that."

Amanda handed her a small bouquet of fresh flowers. "I knew you'd forget these."

"Oh, thank you, Amanda." This was all very nice. But where was Eli? He was nowhere in the room.

## Chapter Nine

Eli was in the restroom splashing his face with cold water. This getting married stuff was harder than he'd thought it would be. Gwen was five minutes late, and he'd been imagining every terrible possibility, from cold feet to car wrecks.

He'd found it impossible to just sit there waiting, so he'd headed down the hall.

The water seemed to help. He wiped his face with a paper towel, combed his hair, then made himself head back to the justice of the peace's office.

On the way, he spotted a man hiding behind a column and watching the door to the judge's chambers. The man wore jeans and a flack jacket. He had a slight build, a pale complexion and curly blond hair. The frayed tie worn loose at his collar seemed like an afterthought.

Most telling was the expensive camera around his neck. Eli would have bet his eyeteeth the man was that troublesome reporter Gwen had warned him about. Harry, Harvey, something like that.

Eli came up behind the reporter and tapped him on

the shoulder. The other man jumped and swiveled around.

"This wedding is private," Eli said evenly. "Haven't you harassed Gwen enough?"

The reporter grinned. "Harassment? Just good investigative reporting. Harvey Brinkman." He held out his hand for Eli to shake.

Eli ignored the hand. "I'm asking you nicely to leave. The bride is in delicate health. She's been ill, and being upset isn't good for her. So do the decent thing and leave us alone."

"Oh, I don't think so. Every time the *Plain Talker* runs a Millionaire, Montana, story, the paper sells out. And almost every single story and picture gets picked up by the wire services, which means a bonus for me. A little bonus might not mean much to rich folks like you, but I'm a struggling reporter and I can barely make my car payments. So let me do my job."

"I'll pay you a hundred bucks to leave the premises."

Harvey drew himself up to his full height, which Eli guessed to be about five foot six. "I cannot be bought, sir. I have my journalistic integrity to think about."

"I've read your stories. You don't have any journalistic integrity. We just have to determine your price. How about two hundred dollars?"

Eli could see the indecision playing on Harvey's face. But then he drew his thin lips into a firm line. "No. I won't do it. And if we're going to start throwing insults, I'd be careful about using words like 'integrity.' It hasn't escaped anyone's notice that you took your time making an honest woman out of Gwen. Maybe an instant family started looking a lot more attractive with a million or so dollars attached.''

It happened before Eli could think. Eli's fist clenched, his arm cocked and he popped Harvey Brinkman right in the nose.

But the reporter was a bit tougher than Eli gave him credit for. He came back swinging, and before Eli could duck Harvey had slammed him in the face with his tape recorder.

Eli saw stars for a moment. His vision cleared just in time to block Harvey's next punch.

''I see I hit a nerve,'' Harvey said with a sneer. ''But what else do you expect people to think? Why else would a man go looking for a one-night stand from months ago, suddenly eager to drag her to the altar?''

Eli pulled back for another punch, but he stopped himself in time. Harvey *wanted* to prolong the fight, maybe acquire a few battle scars, because it would make a better story. Reason enough not to smash the weasel's face in, which was just what Eli was itching to do.

''For the record,'' Eli said through gritted teeth, ''I am marrying Gwen because she is the mother of my children, and because I happen to think she will be an excellent wife. I have a deep and abiding fondness for her.''

Harvey pulled out his notebook and scribbled furiously. ''Fondness. That's not the same as love.''

"I won't mince words with you. Now, are you going to leave, or do I have to call security?"

"This courthouse is a public place. I have as much right to be here as anyone else."

Eli flexed his fist and took a menacing step forward. "Just exactly how expensive is that camera?"

"Are you threatening me with further violence?"

"Just asking a simple question."

"I could file assault charges against you. You threw the first punch."

Eli considered his options. He wasn't really afraid of a minor criminal charge. A good lawyer could get him off with a slap on the wrist, especially given the circumstances. He was defending his pregnant bride's right to some privacy. But the publicity would only cause Gwen more distress, and he didn't want that.

"Three hundred dollars. That's my final offer." It was also all the cash he had in his pocket. He'd been planning to use it to pay for the honeymoon, such as it was.

Apparently he'd found Harvey's price. "You breathe one word about this, and I'll deny it to my death."

"Which might come along sooner than you expect, if you bother us again." Eli pulled a wad of fifties from his wallet and handed them over.

Harvey glanced around to make sure no one was watching, then pocketed the money. "I believe your original request was that I leave the premises. Which I will do. Oh, and Mr. Garrett?"

"What?"

"You're late for your wedding."

Eli looked at his watch. Oh, God, it was eleven-fifteen. He strode toward the J.P.'s chambers and opened the door. "I'm sorry I'm late," he announced, "but I—" He stopped as a collective gasp arose from the assembled guests.

"Eli, what happened?" someone asked.

That's when he saw the blood dripping on his coat sleeve. He glanced into an antique mirror the judge had on his wall and almost fainted. His face was covered with blood. He looked like something out of a horror movie.

Someone handed him a handkerchief, which he used to clean up his face. All of the blood had come from one deep cut on his cheekbone, so it wasn't as bad as it could have been.

"Oh, Eli, you need to have that stitched up." It was Gwen, standing beside him, her face wreathed with concern. "What happened?"

"Harvey Brinkman. When I politely suggested he leave the courthouse rather than upsetting you and endangering your health, he bashed me in the face with his tape recorder."

"How politely?" she asked dubiously, using a Kleenex to dab at the blood he'd missed. "Here, hold this on the cut to stop the bleeding."

"Not very," he admitted. "I hit him first, though not very hard. You're right, he's a very annoying person. But he won't be bothering us any more today."

"You need to go to the emergency room."

"Not until we've said our vows. That's what everyone's here for, right?"

She smiled, and he finally stopped fussing with his bloody face long enough to get a good look at her.

"Oh, my God, Gwendolyn, you look beautiful." With her hair piled up on her head and woven through with flowers, and the flowing green dress, she could have been a goddess.

The goddess of fertility, what else?

"Thank you. I wish I could say the same of you."

"Are we going to have a wedding or not?" Wyla asked crossly.

The woman grated on Eli's nerves any time she opened her mouth. "Yes, we are going to have a wedding." He looked down at Gwen. "We are, aren't we?"

He couldn't quite read her face. Was she concerned? Annoyed? Or disgusted with his back-alley brawling?

Then she smiled. "Yes, we are," she said, and his heart lifted.

IN LIGHT of the circumstances, the J.P. performed the wedding ceremony in record time. Eli gave Gwen a quick kiss on the mouth, which nonetheless left her lips tingling. They signed the marriage license, along with the J.P. and the witnesses, and she became Mrs. Eli Garrett.

After a flurry of hugs and handshakes, congratulations and well wishes, Sylvia took Gwen aside. "Amanda and Shelly and I were going to treat you guys to a wedding reception lunch at the Crystal Ballroom, but—''

''I'm taking Eli to the E.R. Thank you, though, it was nice of you to plan something for us.''

''Even if it's spur-of-the-moment,'' Sylvia said, ''you deserve a nice wedding.''

''It *was* a nice wedding,'' Gwen said, meaning it. ''I thought I just wanted to get through it, but having my friends here means a lot.'' She laid a hand on Eli's arm. ''Eli? You have a date with a suture.''

He wrinkled his nose, making him look like a little boy. ''The bleeding's slowed down a lot. Maybe a butterfly bandage—''

''No dice. I'm not going through the rest of my life known as 'Mrs. Scarface.' Now let's go. Give me the keys to your car, and I'll drive.''

Clearly he didn't want to let her drive his precious Jaguar, but he gave her the keys. She kept a wary eye out for Harvey Brinkman as they exited the courthouse and headed for Eli's car, but he was nowhere in sight. He probably didn't want to take any pictures showing the damage he'd inflicted on Eli.

''Well, that was an interesting wedding,'' Gwen said as she started the engine. It purred to life with a rumble of pure power.

''Are you mad?''

''Mad? Why, because you were throwing your fists around on our wedding day like a schoolyard bully?'' But she softened the question with a smile. ''You were defending me and my right to privacy. You were concerned about me and the babies. What you did was sweet and noble—if a little foolhardy. No, I'm not mad.''

Eli reached over and tucked a flower back into her hair where it had slipped out. ''Thank you.''

The innocent touch sent sparks shooting through Gwen's whole body. She again thought about the wedding night to come and wondered how it would play out.

The emergency room at All Saints wasn't crowded, much to Gwen's relief. She wasn't up to lots of staring from strangers. Her face had become familiar to those following the lottery story, especially here in Pine Run where so many stories had run in the paper and on TV.

''What did the other guy look like?'' the doctor joked as he cleaned the cut on Eli's cheek.

''He got off easy,'' Eli said.

''I wish you'd flattened him,'' Gwen grumbled. ''I'd have gladly paid for you to get out of jail, just to see Harvey Brinkman with a black eye.''

She sat by Eli's gurney, holding his hand to give comfort, though he hadn't asked for it and didn't appear worried or apprehensive. She remembered how he'd done the same thing for her, only a few weeks ago, and smiled. What a couple of tough characters they were.

''Ah, Harvey Brinkman, ace reporter,'' the doctor said, nodding. ''Now I understand.'' He'd put four very neat stitches in Eli's face. ''You might want to have a plastic surgeon take a look at it. You'll definitely have a small scar.''

Eli waved away the doctor's concern. "I was too pretty anyway."

"Are you sure, Eli?" Gwen asked after the doctor left the room. "If money is a problem—"

His laughter cut her off. "No, that's not it. I don't need for you to pay my medical bills."

"It's not a matter of pride, I hope. Because I don't mind."

He released her hand. "Gwen, I have money. Are you telling me you don't know that?"

"Well, yes, that's exactly what I'm telling you. You haven't exactly volunteered to show me your tax returns."

"Is that what that interrogation the other day was all about?"

"Calling it an interrogation is a little rough, don't you think? I was just trying to get some dialogue going. I want us to be able to trust each other—with anything. You can trust me, Eli."

"But do you trust me?" he asked quietly. "Harvey Brinkman seems to think I married you for your money. Is that what you think?"

Gwen wanted to lie. She really, really wanted to lie. But she couldn't, not in the middle of a discussion about trust and honesty. "It crossed my mind, but only when I didn't know you at all. And when you were so willing to sign a pre-nup, well, that pretty much put my mind at ease." *Almost.* "I'm sorry I couldn't just trust you completely right on the spot. I didn't know anything about you except—"

"—except that I was good in bed?"

"Eli! I was going to say, 'except that you were handsome and kind.' Not a bad start, but still, only a start."

"Sorry." Eli shrugged. "They say trust has to be earned, and maybe I haven't earned it yet."

"We'll work it out. If we just talk about things, instead of holding them inside, I know we can make this work."

He took her hand again and squeezed it. "I'm going to try."

They walked to the cashier's station, where Eli was supposed to make his insurance co-payment. He handed the cashier a credit card.

A few moments later, she slid the card back to him. "I'm sorry, Mr. Garrett, but the card's no good."

*"What?"*

"Either you're over the credit limit, or you haven't paid your bill."

"That's impossible. Try it again."

"I already tried it twice," the cashier said with an apologetic tone. "We take personal checks."

Gwen reached into her purse and produced her own credit card. "Here, I'll get it."

"No, you won't. We'll work this out some other way."

But the cashier had already snatched the card away.

"Eli, don't be ridiculous. We're married."

"I could drive back to Jester and get another card. I have a drawer full of them. Or my checkbook."

"If it's important to you, you can pay me back later. I'm not interested in more driving. I'm tired, and I'd like to go to our hotel." Where, hopefully, they could put this entire incident behind them and get on with being married.

"Damn, I wasn't even thinking about you. Do you want to sit down? Can I get you something to drink? I think I might have fifty cents in my pocket."

She grinned. "I'll be off my feet soon enough."

Eli folded his arms. "This is embarrassing, you know."

"Well, a little embarrassment keeps us humble."

"I had three hundred in cash, but I used it to bribe Harvey Brinkman."

"So that's how you got rid of him." Gwen signed the credit card slip and took her receipt. "Well, it was money well spent. Shall we go, Mr. Garrett?"

"As you wish, Mrs. Garrett." He took her arm, and Gwen found she could breathe easily again. Men and their pride. The fact his credit card had been refused didn't mean anything. That happened to innocent people all the time—probably a computer glitch.

She refused to believe it was anything else. She was turning over a new leaf. From this day forward, she would trust Eli completely, unless he gave her a reason not to.

THE HISTORIC Westwind Hotel was small and luxurious, catering to couples who wanted a romantic getaway and business travelers who were used to the best. Gwen had never been inside, and though she'd always heard nice things about the hotel, she was still

a bit surprised a town the size of Pine Run had such
a gem tucked away on the town square.

"Oh, Eli, this is so nice," she said as the bellman
placed their small suitcases on side-by-side luggage
racks. The room was huge and had its own stone fire-
place with gas logs. Oriental rugs covered the pol-
ished oak floor, and a massive four-poster with a can-
opy dominated the far end of the room.

Closer to the door was a sitting area featuring silk-
upholstered overstuffed chairs and a fainting couch.

Gwen couldn't resist the fainting couch. It was surprisingly comfortable. "Oh, yes, I could get used to
this. All I need is a cup of tea and a book to read,
and I'm set."

Eli whispered something to the bellman, who quietly withdrew. Then Eli scooted Gwen's legs over a
bit and sat next to her. "Just what every new husband
wants to hear—that his bride intends to spend their
wedding night reading and sipping tea."

Gwen's heart fluttered, as it did whenever she had
carnal thoughts about Eli, and warm honey flowed
through her veins. She thought he might lean down
to kiss her, but instead he slipped off her shoes and
massaged her feet.

She'd never thought of feet as being an erogenous
zone, but the feel of Eli's strong hands squeezing and
pressing in just the right places, was making her lit-
erally short of breath. All she could think about was
how his hands would feel on other parts of her body.

"You're a god," she said. When he'd thoroughly

massaged her feet, he stood and offered her a hand up.

"Where are we going?"

"To the bed, where we can be more comfortable."

"Eli…did I mention that I can't make love? Not that you'd want to, but I just thought I'd set the terms up-front."

He smiled gently. "You mean you can't have intercourse. But there are lots of ways to make love."

His eyes burned into her, and Gwen could have sworn the temperature went up ten degrees. Just what exactly did he have in mind? She was most anxious to find out.

He helped her up and led her to the bed. "First, I insist you take off your stockings. For your comfort, of course." He gallantly turned his back while removing his jacket and tie.

Gwen was more than happy to dispense with her maternity panty hose. Then she climbed onto the bed, propped some pillows behind her, and waited.

"You don't mind if I get comfortable, too, do you?"

"Oh, be my guest." He peeled off his shirt. Gwen enjoyed the visual feast of his muscular chest and powerful shoulders, tanned from working shirtless while patching the roof of his house.

But he didn't stop there. He unfastened his belt, then shucked his pants and boxers all in one graceful movement.

Gwen knew she should have been shocked, or at least surprised, that he would be so unselfconscious when they hadn't been intimate for months. He hadn't even kissed her today, except for that brief smack after they'd been declared husband and wife.

But she was too fascinated to be shocked. He was the most gorgeous naked man she'd ever seen. All right, granted, she hadn't seen very many, but Eli was anatomical perfection personified—lean and powerful like a racehorse or a tiger.

And he quite definitely desired her! The evidence of his arousal wasn't something he could fake.

Eli climbed onto the bed, crawling toward her on all fours with a predatory gleam in his eye. Gwen's heart did that fluttering thing again. Just what *did* he have in mind?

"I bet you'd like to have the pins out of your hair."

"Oh, yes, that would be divine." She maneuvered so that her back was to him. He placed two pillows behind her for support, then began gently removing the roses from her hair.

With the first bloom, he ran the petals along the nape of her neck before discarding it. He grazed her jaw with the second flower, sending shivers in every direction. Each rose he removed became a teasing caress—on her neck, her throat, the tops of her breasts. He even inched her skirt up and rubbed one of the flowers on her thigh.

"I'm going to be very sad when you run out of flowers," she said, her voice shaking. Did he have any idea what he was doing to her? How much stimulation could one woman stand?

He took out the hairpins next. She hadn't realized

they were poking her in the head until he removed them, massaging each sore spot as he went. Soon the strands of her auburn hair fell around her shoulders, across her face, as Eli rubbed her scalp.

"Where's your hairbrush?" Eli asked. "You've got some tangles."

"In that small black bag," she said, pointing. "But you don't have to—"

"I want to." He slid from the bed and walked over to retrieve her cosmetic bag. She watched his tight buns, the only part of him—from this angle, anyway—unkissed by the sun. Her palms itched to touch them, to see if they were really as hard as they looked. She seemed to recall that they were.

With the bag in hand, he walked around the room, turning off all the lights except for one small lamp. Then he drew the curtains, so that everything was bathed in only the dim golden glow of the low-wattage bulb.

"I've never had a naked man play with my hair before," she commented as he began to gently brush her long hair, one section at a time. He removed tangles one by one until the brush ran smoothly from scalp to the middle of her back. Then he laid the brush aside and combed with his fingers, tracing the tips along her hairline at her nape.

"Promise me you'll never cut your hair short," he said in a coarse voice.

Gwen's hair had always been her finest feature. "I won't cut it."

He massaged her neck and shoulders, unzipping her dress and pushing the velvet aside.

The warmth of his hands on her bare skin sent pleasurable shivers throughout her body.

She said nothing when he unhooked her bra and slid the straps down her arms. The dress was bunched at her waist now—or where her waist would have been if she had one. He caressed her breasts from behind, pulling her against his chest, the rough hair crinkly against her tender skin.

Gwen was both aroused and relaxed. Her nipples beaded against his palms. Pregnancy had made her breasts more sensitive than ever, but Eli's touch was never too firm. He breathed into her ear as his hands migrated downward to caress her belly. He must have sensed her reticence about revealing her entire body to him, even in the low light, because he left her dress where it was, sliding his hands beneath the velvet to run his fingers reverently over her taut skin.

Gwen knew she should be embarrassed. But she was too caught up in the moment to object. No man had ever made her feel so desirable, so beautiful, even when she'd been slender.

She wanted to make love—she really did. But she couldn't possibly.

Eli leaned back, removing the pillows that were bunched between them and urging her to lie against him, spoon fashion. His arousal pressed at the small of her back, reminding her that he would want satisfaction.

"Eli…"

"Just relax. I want to do this for you." His hand slid farther down, to the top of her panties, then under the elastic, and she realized exactly what he had in mind.

Reflexively she parted her legs slightly. She craved release too strongly to worry about the fact she was being a really bad, selfish and lazy lover. That night in Roan, she'd been a wild woman, racking her brain for ways to please Eli, constantly moving, adjusting, finding new positions, new places to kiss, new ways to stroke and tease. Now she lay passively, taking pleasure but not giving it.

When Eli's fingers dipped into the valley between her legs, she moved beyond reason. Every brain cell became devoted to receiving the intense sensations, Eli's clever fingers moving slickly inside her, inexorably finding the exact spot that would drive her insane.

Her peak came quickly. Like a rose bursting into bloom, petals of desire opened and spread in an ever-widening circle, spreading to her limbs, swirling around her heart, then melting into warm honey.

"Oh, Eli, that was…that was…" She couldn't complete the sentence. She couldn't adequately describe what he'd done to her, and anyway, her tongue felt thick and unwieldy.

"Good." He placed a soft kiss on her lips, then her cheek.

Gwen lay there, thinking she should move. Her new husband had just given her an incredibly sensual experience, and she wanted to return the favor. She knew of at least seven ways she could pleasure him. Though it had been a long time, she still remembered all the places he liked to be touched and which caresses made him writhe with pleasure.

But her arms and legs refused to move. She wanted to open her eyes, lift her head and launch a sensual campaign that would convince Eli he hadn't married a dud. But she was losing the battle with the sleep she so craved.

When next she opened her eyes, the room was dark. She was naked under the covers, and Eli was gone.

# Chapter Ten

The image of Gwen awash in pleasure stayed with Eli as he ran his very necessary errands. He knew the wedding and hospital visit had exhausted her. He felt a little guilty about drawing her into any sort of sex play at all, when he should have just encouraged her to rest. But she'd been so lovely, he hadn't been able to keep his hands off her.

He was pleased he'd been able to kindle a fire in her so easily, but she was incredibly responsive, just as he remembered. Though he still thrummed with longing himself, it hadn't exactly been a hardship for him to explore her body in ways she enjoyed. He'd been gratified to watch the ecstasy steal over her, feel the spasms that wracked her body, hear the small, involuntary cries she made in the back of her throat. If he couldn't experience that level of pleasure himself, it was a small price to pay. The last thing he wanted was to make her feel guilty for not being able to accommodate him.

He ran his errands as quickly as possible, hoping to return to the room before Gwen awoke from her nap and wondered where he was. But given their unfortunate history where notes in hotel rooms were concerned, he'd decided to skip that gesture.

His first stop was a bank that had an ATM machine. Though he'd only brought that one useless credit card, he had a debit card for emergencies.

Since he'd withdrawn cash that morning, he could only get two hundred dollars. But that should be enough to tide him over until tomorrow. He'd paid in advance for the hotel with a different card, so at least that was taken care of.

His next stop was the same jewelry store where he'd bought Gwen's wedding ring. He wished he'd thought earlier of buying a wedding gift for Gwen. It hadn't even occurred to him until he'd caught a glimpse of a gold-wrapped gift peaking out of her suitcase. He was no good at buying gifts for women, but he supposed jewelry was as safe a bet as anything.

The clerk showed him several items, but none of them seemed exactly right for Gwen. Then he spied something in a display case. He asked the clerk to unlock the case so he could get a closer look.

Oh, yes, these were perfect. ''I'll take them both.''

''Both?''

''Definitely. And can you wrap them?''

''Certainly, sir.''

She disappeared into a back room for a few minutes, and when she reappeared, she handed him a colorfully wrapped package. He paid for the purchase—a modest price, but in this case Eli believed it was the thought behind the gift that counted. He hurried back to the hotel, found the bellman who had carried their luggage and tipped him double because he'd had to wait, then climbed the stairs two at a time rather than wait for the slow-as-a-glacier elevator.

It amazed him how eager he was to return to his bride. He couldn't remember any woman captivating him so thoroughly. Maybe it was the novelty of suddenly having a wife; maybe it was the fact that Gwen carried his children. He didn't know. His attraction for her was slightly disconcerting for a man who'd adopted "control" and "moderation" as middle names.

Eli found Gwen reclining on the fainting couch with her book and her cup of tea, just as she'd mused about earlier. She wore a gold silk caftan and had left her hair unbound. It cascaded around her shoulders in a reddish-brown halo.

"There you are," she said, her smile appearing a bit forced. "Where have you been?"

"I'm sorry. I thought I'd be back before you woke up. I had to find an ATM or you were going to be footing the bill for the entire honeymoon."

"I told you I didn't mind," she chided him gently. "What law says the man has to pay for everything?"

"Eli's law. Whoever comes up with the idea and makes the arrangements also comes up with the cash."

"Sounds reasonable. What's in the bag?"

Eli figured he might as well get this over with. If it was a bad idea for a gift, he'd soon know it. Gwen wasn't very good at hiding her feelings. He reached inside the small shopping bag and pulled out the gift. Only then did he realize it was wrapped in baby wrap, with little yellow duckies and pink bunnies.

"Uh, this was supposed to be a wedding gift. I didn't specify when I asked for gift wrap."

Gwen's green eyes danced with curiosity. "Oh, Eli, you didn't have to—"

"Don't bother. I know you got something for me, because I saw the package. Anyway, it's nothing much."

"Let's just see about that." She opened the package carefully, then reached into the tissue paper and withdrew the two antique silver baby cups. "Oh, Eli, they're precious."

"When I saw two of them together in the store, I figured it was meant to be. I'll have them engraved."

"With Thing One and Thing Two?"

"I assume we'll come up with better names at some point."

She studied the cups again, then smiled. "These are so sweet. Thank you." She stood and hugged him.

Her nearness, her scent, had an immediate effect on his blood pressure. For the tenth time that day, he reminded himself of her delicate condition.

Gwen went to her suitcase and retrieved the gold-wrapped box. "I wasn't even sure I was going to give it to you. It's kind of silly. But you're very hard to buy for."

"Me? Buy me a new power tool and I'm happy as a clam." But clearly no power tool would fit into such a small box. His curiosity getting the better of him, he ripped into the paper like a little kid on his birthday. When he saw the set of keys, he was confused. Oh, God, she wasn't giving him a car, was she?

"It's a copy of all my keys," she said, her face turning red. "The house, my office, my desk, my private quarters—which are yours, too, now—the garage, my car, everything. The key chain is a jaguar."

"Like my car," he said, feeling a bit slow.

"Oh, Sylvia was right. It's way lame."

Eli laughed with delight, finally getting it. "No, Gwen, it's wonderful. You obviously put a lot of thought into your gift, unlike me, and the gesture means a lot. And the key chain is classy. I'll put my other keys on it right now."

"You don't have to carry it," she said. "You can keep it in a drawer. You won't hurt my feelings."

"Of course I'll carry it, and proudly." As he inspected the key chain more closely, he realized it was made of eighteen-karat gold, and unless he missed his guess, the jaguar's eyes were diamonds. This was no trinket. His heart swelled a bit as he fully absorbed the meaning behind the gift.

She trusted him.

"And, Eli?"

"Yes, Gwen?" He couldn't stop grinning. She was one in a million.

"I'm sorry I fell asleep. You made me feel so wonderful, and I fully intended to…I wanted you to have fun, too." Now her face was definitely red.

He enfolded her in his arms. "You think I didn't enjoy that?"

"You know what I mean."

"I assure you, there will be many opportunities for you to reciprocate, if you so desire, but there's no obligation, no expectation on my part. It can't be that much fun carrying fifty pounds of extra weight, and I just wanted you to feel good."

"Forty pounds! Let's not make it any worse than it already is. And you did make me feel good—better than I've felt since I don't know when. I didn't just feel good, I felt…pretty."

"You *are* pretty—gorgeous, in fact. Any time you want to feel even prettier, just let me know."

GWEN FELT LIKE a princess for the rest of the day. She was starving, so they ordered a sumptuous feast of roast duckling with wild rice and honey-glazed carrots and raspberry truffle cake, all washed down with sparkling white grape juice as a stand-in for champagne. They explored the hotel, which featured hidden alcoves and winding staircases. All of the antiques were for sale, and Gwen purchased several small pieces to round out the boardinghouse furnishings.

Their room had a TV and VCR tucked away in an armoire, and the hotel offered an extensive library of classic films. They chose *Breakfast at Tiffany's,* which Eli had never seen, and Gwen embarrassed herself by crying as she always did when Audrey Hepburn ran after the cat she claimed not to care about.

When bedtime rolled around, Gwen dressed with care in the maternity nightgown Sylvia had bought for her, which was more revealing than Gwen would have chosen for herself. But she was starting to feel less self-conscious about her oddly shaped body, thanks to Eli's attentions.

He was waiting in bed for her when she came out of the bathroom. As promised, he gave her ample opportunity to bring him pleasure, though he certainly didn't neglect her needs. They discovered creative ways to cuddle that Gwen was willing to bet even the *Kama Sutra* didn't include.

When they finally slept, Eli tucked Gwen against him. She was exhausted, but it was a good kind of exhaustion. Though neither of them had used words of love, Gwen *felt* loved. Intellectually she knew sex wasn't the same as true love, and that hormones had a way of confusing the two. Still, she considered their wedding night an important step on the road to the deep and abiding, eternal love she'd always dreamed of finding.

As she drifted off to sleep, she decided that though their marriage had gotten off to an unconventional start, things were looking up.

GWEN AND ELI enjoyed a leisurely breakfast in the Westwind Hotel's dining room. Eli signed it to the room, then checked out. They took a circuitous route home, taking in the fall leaves, which overnight, it seemed, had turned delicious shades of orange and rust. But then their idyllic tryst had to end.

"I probably should have told you before," Eli said

as they crossed the Jester town limits, "but I have to go out of town. To Las Vegas."

"Oh? What for?"

"Business."

"When? For how long?" She realized she was interrogating him, but the idea of being separated from him even overnight when they'd just started to bond was downright upsetting.

"Just a couple of days. I leave tomorrow morning—early."

"Oh." She wanted to ask him what business a mechanic had in Las Vegas, but she knew darn well that if Eli wanted her to know, he'd have volunteered the information. She tried not to feel piqued at the slight. Just because they were married didn't mean Eli wasn't entitled to some privacy.

But, Las Vegas? The Disneyland of Perennial Debtors?

Her thoughts drifted to the scene at the hospital, when Eli's credit card had been refused. Her grandmother had told her stories about Gwen's father going to Las Vegas, a desperate attempt to win the money he'd owed his creditors. He'd met Gwen's mother soon after that debacle, and a new plan for paying off debts had presented itself.

No. She wasn't going to question or doubt Eli. She'd promised him and herself that she would trust him.

"I've been alone a long time, Gwen," Eli said. "For my entire life, I've been responsible to no one but myself. It may take me a while to develop the habit of consulting you about things."

"It's okay. You were right not to bring it up until now. If you'd told me before, I'd have fretted the entire trip."

"Does that mean you'll miss me?"

"Yes, I'll definitely miss you."

"You aren't going to have those babies while I'm gone, are you?"

"I have three weeks to go."

"But if you do go into labor, you can call me on the cell phone. I'll keep it on twenty-four hours a day, and I'll hop the first plane home if I need to."

"The twins aren't going to be born early," she assured him. "I've instructed them to wait, and they're already very obedient children."

Just then one of them gave a particularly emphatic kick, as if objecting to her assessment. Obedient, huh? We'll show her.

Gwen tried to put Eli's upcoming trip out of her mind as she settled in at home. A smattering of wedding gifts had arrived during her absence as news of the marriage had spread, and she had to open those and send thank you cards. She had to open mail, pay bills, answer phone messages. She forced herself to don her walking shoes and take her slow, lumbering laps around the block. Every time she passed Mac's Auto Repair, where Eli was putting the finishing touches on the Nash Coupe he'd been restoring, she drank in the sight of him in his worn-to-white jeans, which looked especially nice when he was bent over with his head in a car engine.

He never noticed her passing.

ELI WOKE UP at four the next morning to make an early flight from Billings. Gwen wanted to get up and make him some breakfast, but he insisted she needed her rest, that he would grab something at the airport. She settled for several drowsy goodbye kisses and a promise to call.

When she awoke several hours later, she found a long note from Eli regarding the Nash. Apparently the owner was on his way to pick up the car. Eli needed for Gwen to collect a cashier's check for twenty-three thousand dollars before turning over the classic car's keys.

*Twenty-three thousand dollars?* For the Bucket o'Bolts? That seemed an unrealistic sum for a car that didn't even have air conditioning. Still, she was relieved to see that Eli had income coming in. It made her worries over his financial situation seem silly.

When the mail arrived, Gwen noticed an envelope addressed to Eli at his Denver address, then stamped with all sorts of forwarding notices. It appeared the mutilated envelope had taken a side trip to Tampa, Florida before finding its way to Jester. And unless Gwen missed her guess, the envelope contained a credit card statement. That would explain why his card had been refused. He probably hadn't paid the bill because he hadn't seen it. The same thing had happened to Sylvia once when her bill had been eaten by a post office sorting machine.

She was glad to have that mystery solved.

Gwen set the bill on her desk, then noticed that the flap was open.

She knew she shouldn't. But she just couldn't resist a small peek.

The balance was over sixteen thousand dollars.

Okay, no reason to panic. The payment from the car buyer would more than cover the debt. And this was none of her business anyway! Or was it? Now that they were married, his debt became her debt.

Still, she tried very hard to put it out of her mind. Debt was the American way. She'd read somewhere that the average American owed eight thousand dollars on credit cards. Just because Eli ran up his credit cards didn't mean he was a candidacy for bankruptcy. All it meant was that they approached their finances differently, and they would have to reach a compromise.

Or she could pay the bill herself.

Eli would have a fit, she thought as she got out her checkbook. But the interest and late charges mounting up over this one bill were no doubt hideous. Each day the bill went unpaid, the debt grew. She wouldn't miss the money, and Eli could pay her back if he wanted. In fact, she was sure he would want to. She wrote the check, stuck it in the envelope, added a stamp, and put it with the outgoing mail before she could think more about it.

Later that day, the Nash customer showed up. He

was a gruff and unpleasant sort, and he wasn't pleased that Eli wasn't there personally to give him the car. He spent a ridiculous amount of time going over the car, then insisted on a test drive.

Gwen thought that was reasonable. She would never buy a car without driving it. So she let him have the keys.

He was gone almost half an hour, and when he came back, he didn't want to pay the full price he'd agreed to.

"There's a scratch on one of the whitewalls," he complained. "And I told Eli I didn't want that rear reflector."

"It's illegal, not to mention unsafe, to drive the car without one," Gwen explained, though she was sure Eli had already done so.

The man grumbled some more, but finally handed over a check for the agreed-upon amount. But it was drawn on his personal account, rather than the cashier's check Eli had specified.

"My husband specifically said it had to be a cashier's check," she told him.

"Are you saying you think my check's no good?"

"I'm not saying anything except that I want to follow my husband's instructions."

"Well, you can take this check, little lady, or I'm walking away from the deal. I know a guy up in Seattle has a better Nash than this for a lot less money."

Gwen started to tell the man to go for it. She knew he was blowing smoke. But what if she was wrong? She would blow Eli's deal, and he might really need that money. So she caved in. If anything went wrong with the check, she would take responsibility for it.

Wracked with guilt, she called Eli on his cell phone and told him what she'd done.

"Don't worry about it," Eli said. "I'd have probably done the same thing. So how are you feeling?"

"Fine, but I miss you."

"I miss you, too," he said, his voice husky. "I'm thinking of catching the red-eye. If I do, I'll be home before you wake up tomorrow."

Gwen thought about waking up in Eli's arms and shivered with anticipated pleasure. "That would be really nice."

That evening, some of her friends surprised her with a baby shower. They just showed up en masse on her front porch, so she didn't have to go out, which was nice.

"I know you can buy anything you need," said Sylvia, who had organized the event. "But we had to do something. I mean, twins! We've never had twin babies in Jester."

"It has nothing whatever to do with the fact that you're special and we love you," Amanda added.

"Come on, now, open your gifts," said Olivia. "Mine first."

The presents they gave her were thoughtful and one-of-a-kind—or in some cases, two-of-a-kind. Finn Hollis, who liked to whittle, had carved mobiles for her to hang over the cribs. Stella had crocheted two miniature afghan blankets. Oggie had gotten some of the students at the school to collaborate on an illustrated children's book.

"You guys are the best friends anyone could hope for," Gwen said with tears in her eyes. "I'm sorry Eli isn't here to share in this."

"We didn't realize he was going out of town," said Wyla, who had somehow wangled an invitation. And, to her credit, she'd given Gwen an adorable ceramic switchplate for the nursery light switch. "Where'd he go?"

"Las Vegas," Gwen said.

"What's he doing there?" Wyla persisted.

It was embarrassing for Gwen to admit she had no idea. Shelly came to the rescue by deftly changing the subject, but Gwen realized it was abnormal for a husband to be so secretive about his business travel. She could tell her friends thought it odd she'd been left in the dark.

But it was like he said, she reasoned later that night as she tried to sleep. He'd never been accountable to anyone but himself. Trust would come slowly. But it would come, she was sure of it. Meanwhile, she had better stop being so suspicious. Nothing could undercut a relationship like unfounded suspicion.

When she awoke the next day, the first thing she saw were two enormous white teddy bears sitting at the foot of the bed. She thought for a moment she was dreaming about the North Pole, until she saw Eli grinning at her.

"I saw them at the airport and I couldn't resist,"

he said before pulling her into his arms for a good-morning kiss.

Apparently there were several things he couldn't resist. Some he'd brought home with him—clothes and toys and games for the girls that they wouldn't be ready to play with for years. Some were delivered by FedEx and UPS—a swing set, tricycles, boxed sets of Disney DVDs.

"Eli, we don't even have a DVD player."

"Oh, yes, we do." That was the next delivery. "Do you think we should get them puppies? Maybe a couple of golden retrievers."

"Oh, yes, that's *all* we need is two puppies to care for in addition to two babies. Eli, get a grip, please!" But she couldn't help laughing. She'd wanted a caring and involved father, and so far she wasn't disappointed. Granted, buying presents was a lot easier than changing a diaper at four in the morning, but Eli's generosity was a good sign.

She hoped he wasn't overextending himself, but she'd vowed to stay out of his finances, and she tried very hard to do that.

Unfortunately, the cheery bubble of matrimonial bliss and expectant-parent rapture came to an abrupt end.

Gwen was baking cranberry muffins. She'd been feeling exceptionally energetic today, and now that the summer heat was but a memory she'd felt like having a meaningful relationship with her oven. Eli, still in his work clothes, wandered into the kitchen and got himself a beer from his private stash in the fridge. Since he never overindulged, Gwen had decided to lift her grandmother's ban on alcohol.

Eli didn't greet her with his customary smile and kiss.

"Eli, is something wrong?"

"Nothing that can't be fixed with a barrel of money."

*"What?"*

"Bud Farrell, the guy who bought the Nash?"

"Yes?"

"He stopped payment on the check. Apparently on his way back to Denver he had an accident—totaled the car. He claims it was the car's fault—my fault— and he's threatening to file suit."

Gwen set down the pan of muffins she'd just removed from the oven and joined Eli at the table. "That's terrible! What can we do?"

*"We* won't do anything. It's not your problem. I'll take care of it."

"But I'm the one who accepted the wrong kind of check. Anyway, we're married. That means we share our problems."

"Don't worry, he can't get to your money. You're protected by the pre-nup."

"I don't care about that. I'm asking how I can help."

He took a long swallow of beer. "The lawyers will hash it out. Mr. Farrell doesn't have a legal leg to stand on. He was driving with inadequate insurance, even though he assured me he had plenty. Now he's trying to weasel out of having to pay me, that's all. I doubt he'll sue me if I let it drop.''

''But you'll be out all that money! You worked hard for that.''

''Or, I can turn lawyers loose on him. I'll get my money, along with a huge bill for legal services. Either way I've been screwed over.''

''I feel very responsible. Let me pay for the lawyer.''

She thought he would be grateful, even if he turned her down. Instead he struck like a snake. ''I don't need your money! What do I have to do to convince you of that?''

Gwen took an instinctive step backward. ''Well, excuse me for trying to help.'' She got up and went back to her muffins, keeping her back to Eli, hoping, praying he would apologize. Instead, she heard his chair scrape back and his footsteps leaving the kitchen.

''Dammit,'' she muttered as her eyes filled with tears. She dumped the muffins into a cloth-lined basket and covered them for later. How could there be any hope for their marriage if Eli wouldn't talk to her about anything important? He was big on buying gifts for the babies, but he obviously didn't see Gwen as a real partner.

She was just the mother of his children.

## Chapter Eleven

The Tanner Boardinghouse became an armed camp. For two days, Gwen and Eli barely said a word to each other. But she was determined she was not going to apologize for offering help. He was being ridiculous!

Meals were an ordeal to be survived. Oggie, Irene and Stella tried to engage the unhappy couple in conversation, but if Gwen and Eli talked at all, it was in monosyllables, and never to each other.

Nights were the worst. Another cold front had come through, and Gwen would dearly have loved to snuggle up to her husband for warmth, instead of relying on a down comforter. But Eli slept on the very edge of his side of the bed, his back turned to her. She thought his behavior was very juvenile, and she wanted to tell him so. But that would only make things worse.

There was something about Eli's demeanor that bothered her. He wasn't just mad, he was hurt. Her offer of financial assistance had injured his pride, apparently. But the hurt seemed to be bone-deep, and

Gwen was sure there was something going on besides his dented male ego.

On the morning of the third day, just when things couldn't get any worse, they did. As she was helping Irene with the breakfast dishes, Eli barreled into the kitchen with a face that looked like a thundercloud.

"Eli, what is it?"

Irene took one look at him, mumbled some excuse and scooted out of the kitchen.

"I just got off the phone with my credit card company," Eli said.

Uh-oh. She had some explaining to do. At least he was talking to her.

"You opened my mail?" he demanded.

"It was already open. The post office did a number on the envelope. And you were out of town, and I was worried about that balance being overdue—I didn't want your credit to be ruined. After all, it's my credit, too."

"And it didn't occur to you to call me first? Ask me what to do? Or at least tell me what you'd done?"

She hadn't because she'd known he wouldn't be pleased. A few days ago, they'd been having so much fun being newlyweds and preparing for the babies that she hadn't wanted to spoil things. Then, after their argument, she'd figured it would be matrimonial suicide to confess she'd paid his bill. She'd just hoped he wouldn't notice, that he wouldn't remember how large the balance had been.

"I'm sorry, Eli, truly I am. Credit card debt makes me very uneasy."

"I had it under control," he said, teeth clenched. "Gwen, a fistful of keys means nothing if you don't really trust me."

"Maybe I would trust you more if you trusted me! You acted all secretive about your business trip."

"If you wanted to know about my business trip, why didn't you ask me? Am I supposed to be a mind reader?"

"I was raised not to be nosy. But I'm asking now."

"I was gambling away the grocery money."

Gwen's eyes filled with tears. "Just forget it." She swept past him and headed for the stairs, wishing desperately that she could run. But the size she was, lumbering was the best she could do.

Eli was right behind her. "Gwen, wait. I'm sorry. You asked a question, and you deserve an honest answer."

"I already knew that," she said through her tears. "Eli, just go away. I'm going to cry for a while, and I want to do it alone."

ELI BACKED OFF, but only because he didn't want to make things worse. He would give Gwen a chance to calm down and cool off. Meanwhile, he would do a little cooling off himself.

Was paying his credit card balance such a terrible thing? Had he overreacted?

Eli sank onto the stairs, propped his chin in his hands, and gave it a good long think. Most men would be overjoyed to have a rich wife pay off his bills. But the fact was, Eli liked to do things himself. That was why he'd done well with his business. He relied on no one but himself. He didn't have to worry about a payroll, or whether he could trust his employees, or whether his workers were doing things exactly as he would do them.

That was why he was renovating the house next door with his own hands, rather than hiring a contractor. When he looked at a smooth wood floor or a flawless paint job, he could say, *I did that.* And if he messed up a job, if it wasn't perfect, he could tear it out and start over without answering to anyone.

When he took help from someone, they expected something in return. Or they pitied him, saw him as a charity case. He didn't care for either scenario. What did Gwen expect? She had his loyalty, his affection and his promise to be the best father he knew how to be. Was she worried he would grow bored with family life and leave? Was she trying to tie him to her with gratitude?

Or did she merely see him as a charity case, someone she could rescue and rehabilitate with her money?

He rubbed his eyes. It hurt to think about these things. He'd never imagined a relationship with a woman could be so complicated. Of course, his other relationships—if they could even be called that—had been simple to walk away from.

He cocked his head and listened for any noise coming from upstairs, but all was quiet. He decided a peace offering was in order, He went to the kitchen and brewed a cup of Gwen's favorite raspberry tea, then poured it into a pretty blue-and-white china cup. He carried it carefully up the stairs and knocked on the bedroom door.

"Gwen?"

There was no answer, so he went inside. She was lying on the bed, on top of the covers, sound asleep. Her face was puffy from crying, and a twinge of guilt arrowed through Eli's heart. Part of him wanted to stay mad at her. It was so much more comfortable keeping her a safe distance from his heart.

But, God, look at her! How could he continue to hurt her, no matter how much righteous indignation he wrapped around himself?

He smoothed a strand of her glorious auburn hair off her cheek. She stirred, opened her eyes and immediately tensed. He hated the wariness in her eyes. It was the look of a dog that was expecting to be kicked.

"I brought you some tea."

She sat up and propped herself up with pillows. "Thank you." She took the cup and sipped at the tea, her gaze never leaving him.

"I was in Las Vegas consulting with some developers who are building a new casino with an automotive theme. They've acquired some old cars with historical significance—cars belonging to famous gangsters, complete with bullet holes. The car some movie star died in."

"Oh, that's really macabre."

"That's what I told them. They didn't care. They're

looking for someone to restore the cars in a certain way—to pretty them up while leaving visible damage.''

Gwen wrinkled her nose. ''I hope you demanded a high fee. A distastefulness bonus.''

''It's not the kind of business I'm interested in.''

''You turned it down?''

''I told them I'd restore the cars nobody had died in. They told me I was superstitious.'' He laughed and shook his head. ''They're going with a bigger outfit that can work faster and cheaper.''

''I'm sorry.''

''Don't be. I stopped by the black jack table on my way out of town and won two thousand dollars.'' He went to the dresser, opened a drawer, and pulled out a package.

''More presents for the girls?''

''For all of us. And something for you.'' He'd been thinking about the fact that his ''wedding present'' to Gwen had really been a gift for the babies. He should have gotten her something more personal.

Gwen opened the box as if she expected something to jump out and bite her. But when she saw the book of baby names, she smiled. ''Amanda will be mad you didn't buy this from her.''

''She'll survive. Look under the book.''

Gwen gasped when she saw the diamond stud earrings nestled in the cotton. ''Oh, Eli, you shouldn't blow money on such expensive presents.''

''But it was a windfall.''

''And it could have just as easily been a huge loss.

Why would you gamble? Why would anyone want to gamble?''

"This, coming from a woman who won the lottery?''

Gwen smiled and turned pink. "You're right. Although a dollar a week is hardly gambling. But I guess it's none of my business if you want to spend your money that way. Thank you for the earrings. They're beautiful.'' She took a sip of tea, then changed the subject. "Remember, I told you my mother was a Rhymann?''

"Yeah, sure.''

"Well, she really was a mustard heiress. Her grandfather left her a big chunk of change when he died. Anyway, my father lured my mother into marriage by pretending he was a prosperous rancher. What he really was, was a pig farmer, and not a very good one.''

Eli waited, sensing Gwen had a point to make here.

"My father was a gambling addict. Within months of their marriage, he'd wiped out my mother's bank account by paying off some rather unsavory characters he owed money to. She was ready to forgive him, if he promised to stop gambling. But he couldn't, and he left her with a pile of new debts—and me.''

Aw, jeez. No wonder she was a little sensitive about money issues. No wonder his sudden trip to Las Vegas had sent her bouncing off the walls.

"I don't even like gambling that much,'' he assured her. "Anyway, I would never gamble more than I could afford to lose.''

"But you were counting on that twenty-three thousand dollars from the Nash."

"I don't spend money until it's in the bank."

"But the credit card—"

"I pay it off every month."

"You spent sixteen thousand dollars in one month?"

"I had to buy building supplies, and equipment for the garage. A new furnace. Stained glass for the front door. It adds up. Gwen, please, I'm a big boy. I can handle my money."

"But you haven't always, have you?"

The air in the room seemed to change texture. A new tension, a dangerous one, sprang up between them.

"I know about your bankruptcy," she said quietly, though she might as well have been screaming the words. "And you had your name changed. What was that all about?"

Eli stared at her for a few excruciatingly slow heartbeats as the meaning of her words sank in. "What did you do, hire a private investigator?"

"No, I—"

"I don't want to hear any more excuses. Gwen, if you had doubts about me, why in hell did you marry me?" With that he walked out of the bedroom, slamming the door.

GWEN COULD HAVE kicked herself around the block. Why had she brought up the bankruptcy? Damn

Bobby Larson for telling her about it in the first place. She'd have been much better off not knowing.

She and Eli had been making progress. They'd been talking, really communicating. He hadn't even been defensive when he'd explained to her how he'd spent all that money. Then she'd blown it by mentioning the bankruptcy.

Shoot, shoot, shoot! Things were going to be worse than ever.

She rubbed her swollen belly, impatient for her babies to arrive, though she knew the longer they stayed inside her, the stronger and healthier they'd be. Maybe when she gave birth, she and Eli would pull together for the common cause. No matter how angry he was with her, she couldn't see him abandoning his children. He'd seemed too enamored with the idea of becoming a daddy. He'd bought that book of baby names, and the floor of the nursery was about to collapse with the weight of all the baby gear he'd brought home.

She picked up the baby book and flipped it open, caught by surprise by the inscription: *For my darling and very pregnant Gwen. I believe we can do better than "Thing One" and "Thing Two." Your husband, Eli.*

Gwen's heart gave a lurch. That was about as sentimental as Eli had ever gotten. She stared at the word "darling" for many long moments. Eli had never called her darling before. She grinned as she thought about showing her daughters the inscription when they were old enough to read. But the grin turned to a frown.

*"This is what your father wrote before he started to hate me."* At the rate they were going, he would never call her darling again, much less tell her he loved her.

Eli wasn't anywhere in the house when Gwen roused herself for dinner. But she heard hammering next door, relentless pounding that had her wincing with every blow.

"You're still not talking?" Stella asked as she passed Gwen some mashed potatoes.

"We started to. But then I blew it again. I just seem to do everything wrong."

"It takes two to disagree," said Irene.

"Eli should make more allowances for you," Oggie added. "You're pregnant, after all. Stella, can I pass you the cornbread?"

"Yes, Oggie, thank you." Was that a blush in Stella's cheeks? Was it possible Stella had finally, *finally* noticed that Oggie carried a torch for her?

Gwen would dearly love to see two of her favorite people get together. Of course, if they did, they would probably move out. As newlyweds, they would want to set up housekeeping in their own place. The loss of income for Gwen would mean little, but she would miss their companionship.

But she was jumping the gun. All Stella had done was smile and blush.

By the time Gwen went to bed, Eli still hadn't returned home. She saw lights on at the house next door, though. A chill wiggled up her spine as she wondered whether Eli was accelerating his renovations so he could move out of the boardinghouse.

Surely it wouldn't come to that. This was merely one of those adjustments that newlyweds had to make.

Gwen tried to believe that when she woke up in the middle of the night and found herself still alone in bed. She was hungry and decided to venture downstairs to raid the fridge, a bad habit she'd developed lately. She found Eli asleep on the sofa in her small living area, sprawled in an uncomfortable-looking position.

If he didn't want to sleep with her, he could have returned to his room on the first floor. It would have been much more comfortable. But he'd stayed in their quarters, which must mean something.

Gwen retrieved a huge, fluffy afghan from the linen cupboard and covered Eli with it. Then she sat in her rocking chair and watched him sleep. She watched him a long, long time, wondering how to escape from the pit she'd dug herself into.

The next morning, Eli showered and left the house early, while Gwen was still asleep. When she awoke, she found a terse note explaining he'd gone to Denver on personal business and wouldn't be back until after dinner.

Personal business. He still wasn't going to open up to her.

Early that afternoon, she got a call from her bank. ''There have been three fairly large checks drawn on

your account,'' John Timms, her banker, explained.
''The numbers are out of sequence, and the signature
isn't yours. We'd like you to come to the bank and
help us straighten everything out.''

''Yes, of course, I'll come right now.''

Gwen tried to believe this was all just a silly mistake, that she would get to the bank and discover
she'd made an error and it was completely innocent.
But the sense of dread that plagued her all the way
to Pine Run grew stronger with every mile.

ELI HAD DRIVEN to Denver because he had a sales
contract on his house, and he needed to sign papers.
He hesitated only briefly before signing his name,
knowing this meant there was no going back. Kind
of like the Spanish conquistador who'd arrived in the
New World and ordered his ships burned, so he
couldn't return to his homeland. He was committed
to living in Jester and continuing his business there,
though he wouldn't get as many customers located so
far from a large business center.

He supposed he didn't really care about that. He
had more money saved than he could ever spend, and
lately his consulting work was paying most of the
bills. He'd only been taking on the hands-on resto-
rations that were fun and challenging—like the Nash
Coupe, dammit. It chapped his hide that his painstaking restoration had been undone by one careless turn.

He wanted to live in Jester to be close to his daughters. Even if he and Gwen couldn't make a go of their
marriage—and it was looking more and more that

way—he still intended to be closely involved in raising his children.

As he was leaving Denver, he spotted an FAO Schwartz and couldn't help pulling into the parking lot. He couldn't imagine what was left to buy for his already spoiled daughters, but he looked anyway.

Nothing seemed right. Frustrated, he left the toy store and wandered into the Mommy & Me store next door. A bevy of young mothers and two pregnant women stared at him as he intruded on the female den, but he didn't care.

Swimsuits. That was something the babies didn't have. Calculating how old they would be when next summer rolled around, he looked at the choices for nine and twelve months. He found two styles that matched, gingham checks with ruffles on the butt. They were cute as hell. He pictured two baby girls with Gwen's reddish curls, playing in the wet sand at the beach.

Unfortunately, Gwen was in the picture, too, wearing a sleek swimsuit, the slender figure he remembered restored, her legs long and tanned. Ah, hell. Why couldn't he stop wanting her when she continued to shove him away with her mistrust? But again he found himself wanting to forgive her, wanting to make allowances for her behavior, wanting to give her one more chance.

An older woman with a pinched face rang up his purchases. As he signed his name to the credit card slip, she pushed her glasses on top of her head and stared at him. "You're the—oh, my goodness, you're the guy who married that pregnant millionaire!'' She then clamped her hand over her mouth. ''I'm sorry, I'm so sorry. That was incredibly rude.''

Eli chafed at the attention. He was well-known among classic car enthusiasts, but he wasn't used to being recognized on the street. ''That's okay,'' he forced himself to say. ''May I have my receipt?''

''Oh, yes, of course. How exciting that Fortune's Twins will be wearing clothes from my shop! That's what the media is calling the babies, you know.''

He was unfortunately aware of the nickname. He hoped to hell it would be forgotten before Thing One and Thing Two were old enough to hear it and understand it.

''Could you send me a picture of the babies wearing the swimsuits? I could frame it and put it right by the register.'' She gasped as a new brainstorm hit. ''Or I could use it in my advertising! Maybe they could pose for a professional photographer.''

It was all Eli could do not to snatch his purchases out of the woman's hands and stalk out. ''We don't want any further publicity,'' he said.

Crestfallen, the woman handed Eli his bag, and he departed.

Terrific. He was no longer Eli Garrett, antique car restoration specialist. He was the pregnant millionaire's husband. Soon to be ex-husband, if things continued on as they were.

During the drive back to Jester, Eli wracked his brain for some way to fix what was broken. But it wasn't like a crumpled fender, which he could hammer and sand and paint until it looked like new. Nothing was going to heal his marriage as long as Gwen didn't trust him.

So how did he go about earning her trust?

Then it hit him. Trust was something Gwen couldn't automatically give, not when her own father had betrayed her mother in such spectacular fashion. And maybe trust *should* be earned. He certainly didn't automatically trust his clients, even if they shared a mutual love and appreciation of classic cars. He required contracts and cashier's checks. Once he worked with a client several times, he might do business on a handshake basis.

Gwen had no basis on which to trust him. He'd certainly never provided evidence of his trustworthiness. He'd simply expected her to trust him. And she *had* married him, which indicated at least some degree of trust.

As he drew closer to Jester, he decided he would turn over a new leaf. She'd opened up to him about her painful past. He would do the same. Maybe if she understood something about his past, it would help her to understand *him*—and to believe him when he said he wouldn't do anything to hurt her.

But he wasn't sure he could do it. If she doubted him again, it would crush his soul.

AT THE Pine Run National Bank & Trust three blocks away, Gwen sat in John Timms office, staring in disbelief at the three checks in front of her, all drawn on her money market account, which she seldom used.

One was for seven hundred dollars and change, to a building supply store. The second was to an automotive store, for several more hundred. The third was to a jewelry store, for thirty-seven hundred.

None of them bore her signature, but the illegible scrawl was one she knew well. She'd seen it on her marriage license.

"I take it by the expression on your face you didn't authorize these purchases," John said.

"What? Oh—oh, yes, I did. I just forgot. The signature is my husband's. Eli Garrett. We just got married."

"I'm not showing that your husband is a signatory on your account."

"He will be. We just haven't had time to come in and do the paperwork. I'm sorry to have caused all this trouble. I'll tell him not to sign on my account until he's officially authorized. It's just that, in my condition, it's been hard for me to get out…"

John was automatically contrite. "And I'm sorry for dragging you out today. So you want us to pay these checks?"

She swallowed, her mouth suddenly dry. "Yes." She didn't want Eli to go to jail. She didn't want any legal hassles. She would tell him she didn't intend to have him prosecuted—so long as he got out of her life and stayed out.

"I'm…I'm not feeling too well," she said. "Could you call me a cab?" She could send Stella and Oggie to pick up her car later.

"Certainly, Mrs. Garrett."

"And I'd like to have copies of those checks, if you don't mind. Eli didn't write down the amounts— I'll have to get on him about that."

"Of course."

The taxi arrived in a few minutes. Gwen climbed into the back seat, her legs shaking, clutching three photocopies.

Eli met her at the front door. "Gwen, honey, I've been so worried. Stella said you took off like a bat out of hell, didn't tell anyone where you were going. I was afraid you'd gone into labor or something."

"I'm fine," she said tightly, brushing past him, avoiding the hug he tried to give her.

"Where's your car? Why are you in a taxi?"

She didn't answer as she unbuttoned the maternity coat she'd been forced to buy. Her hands shook so badly she popped one of the buttons. She shoved the coat into the coat closet.

"Gwen, I know you're angry, and I don't blame you. I shouldn't have come down on you so hard. I guess I don't blame you for wanting to check me out—"

"I didn't have you checked out. And if you'd stuck around to talk, you'd have realized that. Bobby Larson is the one who snooped into your past without my knowledge. But I couldn't stop him from telling me what he found out."

Now he really felt like a heel. "I'll explain it all, if you'll give me another chance. Here, I got you these." He opened a long, white box that had been sitting on the coatrack near the door and withdrew the hugest bouquet of roses Gwen had ever seen. He held them out to her.

The sight of all those roses was overwhelming, the scent cloying, suffocating. She took them in her grasp. And then she did something that surprised her as well as Eli. She swung the whole bouquet over her shoulder and whapped him in the head with it. Red and white petals flew through the air and drifted down around them, snow and blood.

"How dare you! How dare you try to pacify me with a bunch of lousy roses. Did you pay for them with one of my checks?"

"Excuse me?"

"Oh, you were clever. I might not have noticed for weeks, because you took the checks from the back of the book. But thank goodness I have a bank that pays attention."

"Have you lost your mind completely?"

She reached into her purse and pulled out the photocopies, now wrinkled and stained with her tears. "I suppose you're going to tell me you know nothing about these?"

## Chapter Twelve

Eli studied first one, then another of the three sheets of paper Gwen had handed to him. But he couldn't make any sense of them. He'd never done business at Builder's Corner. He'd bought lots of things from Tinker's Automotive, but he'd certainly never paid with one of Gwen's checks. And he'd never heard of Byrd's Fine Jewelry.

Still, he couldn't deny that the signature looked like his.

"You actually think I would steal your money?" he demanded.

She shrugged. "I'm sure you didn't think of it that way. After all, we're married."

"It's stealing, and you believe I did it."

"That *is* your signature."

"It looks like my signature, but it isn't."

"No one but you has access to my office, where I keep that checkbook. No one but you has a *key!*"

"Are you kidding? You leave your keys lying around all the time. Anybody could use them."

"Are you suggesting Stella or Irene or Oggie—

that's ridiculous! I've known them all since I was born!''

''And you've known me only a short while. So naturally I'm the guilty one.''

''Eli, it's your signature! And who else around here buys building supplies and automotive supplies and…and jewelry.'' Her eyes filled with tears. ''I can't believe you would buy me a gift with my own money.''

''So I'm tried, convicted and hanged, huh? And Gwendolyn Tanner is judge, jury and executioner.''

Gwen's shoulders drooped. She looked suddenly exhausted, defeated. ''I can't talk about this right now. I've had enough for one day. Please ask Stella or Irene to bring a tray up to me for dinner.''

Sure, he'd deliver her request. Right before he moved out. He didn't have to take this, not from anyone, and certainly not from his wife.

''GWEN, HONEY, this is not good for you,'' Sylvia said, perched on the edge of Gwen's bed. ''You need to get out of this room, get some fresh air. You need to do something with your hair.'' She picked up one dull, lank piece of Gwen's hair, then let it drop onto her shoulder.

''I can't,'' Gwen said on a moan. ''I don't want anyone to see me like this. I swear, I've gained another ten pounds in the past few days. My face is all puffy, my eyes are red and my hair—I can't make it behave. All the body has gone out of it.''

''I can't do anything about your weight,'' Sylvia

said. "I'm afraid only childbirth is going to cure that. But the face and the hair I can fix. Why don't you come into the shop? I have all afternoon free. I can give you a facial, an herbal wrap and a body wave. I'll ask Shelly to bring us a whole chocolate pie."

Gwen gave a desperate little giggle despite her misery. "I'd probably eat the whole thing, too."

"Or we could do salads and bran muffins, you know, the whole health nut thing. It'll be just like a spa. C'mon, Gwen. I hate seeing you like this."

Gwen knew her grieving hermit act had everyone worried. Stella, Irene and Oggie had been hovering over her, three diligent mother hens plying her with herbal tea, hot chocolate and chicken soup. A steady stream of her friends had stopped by. Everyone had heard, of course, that Eli had left her.

He'd moved out the day of their argument, into his house next door. His close proximity was one of the reasons she didn't want to leave the house, or even her room. She was afraid she would run into him and make some terrible scene.

"All right," Gwen finally agreed. "I do need to get out and breathe some fresh air, if only for the babies' sake. Anyway, my back is killing me from lying around in bed."

"Atta girl. We'll have a total, self-indulgence pity party. You can bad mouth your husband, and I can just slam men in general."

But she didn't really want to say nasty things about Eli. She hadn't told anyone but Sylvia the reason for their breakup. Whenever she thought of their argument, she remembered the terrible anger in his eyes, and the hurt. He felt betrayed by her lack of trust, even when he'd just proved he couldn't be trusted.

What Eli had done was the symptom of a problem. A pretty serious problem, but still, she had spoken those words, "for better, for worse." Maybe her sudden wealth had made her a more attractive bride, but she was sure that wasn't the only reason he'd married her. No man could fake the affection he'd shown her, the concern for her physical condition or the heady anticipation he'd shown regarding the twins' impending birth. She was sure that deep down he was a good man. And if he had a gambling addiction or merely a spending problem, maybe together they could tackle it.

But there was little chance of that, she realized. The gulf between them had grown too large and she had no idea how to breach it.

Gwen put on her favorite maternity outfit, a sage-green sweater over matching leggings. The color reminded her of her wedding dress. If she was going to wallow in her misery, might as well go all the way.

She and Sylvia stopped in at The Brimming Cup to have lunch—rich tomato soup with chili-mac, real comfort food. The meal was such an indulgence, Gwen didn't feel she needed the chocolate pie. Which was a good thing, since the babies were sitting on her stomach.

The next stop was The Crowning Glory, where Sylvia gave Gwen the works—manicure, pedicure, facial.

"What would you think about me opening a spa?" Sylvia asked idly as she applied a final clear coat of polish to Gwen's fingernails.

"In Jester?"

"Sure, in Jester, or close by. I'd have to build, but what else am I going to do with my money? I don't have any kids' college tuition to save for."

"But you might have them, some day. Do you want kids?"

Sylvia shrugged. "I used to. But after watching you and Shelly go through your pregnancies, I'd have to think twice." She laughed. "Besides, I'd like to get married first, and I've never met a guy that even tempted me in that direction. Men are just…they're just turds. They're fun as long as I can walk away from them and go home alone."

"But alone is so…lonely. I don't know what I'd do without Stella and Irene and Oggie."

"I don't mind my own company. And I like my freedom. When you're single, you have this amazing world of possibilities open to you. You can move anywhere, date anybody, have sex, not have sex, dye your hair blue, behave like an idiot with no one to answer to. But the minute you say 'I do,' all the choices close up."

"It's a trade off," Gwen agreed. "But since I never wanted to live anywhere else—or dye my hair blue, for that matter—I didn't notice I was giving anything up. I was gaining a life partner. The security of knowing I had someone to grow old with." Gwen's eyes teared up. "But I guess that was just an illusion."

"Now, Gwen, don't cry. You'll melt your facial mask. What do you think about the spa? Really?"

Gwen sniffed back the tears. She sensed Sylvia wanted a serious answer, so she gave it some thought before answering. "If you made it really special, you could attract customers from all over the northwest."

"That's what I was thinking! With all the improvements in town, and if Bobby Larson builds his hotel, Jester could become the Jackson Hole of Montana. And a luxury spa would fit right in."

"Are you in favor of Bobby's hotel?" Gwen asked, surprised.

"If he could find the right place to build it. Not the park, and not your property. I'd strangle him if he tried to tear down any of our Victorians. But tourism might not be such a bad thing for Jester. Let's face it, the town was dying around us before the lottery saved it."

Gwen knew Sylvia was right. But Bobby Larson's constant carping about tourism and progress, out with the old, in with the new, got on Gwen's nerves. She didn't want a shopping mall that would drive The Mercantile out of business, or a cineplex that would do the same for Pop's Movie Theater. Jester might be old-fashioned, but it was comfortable and familiar, and the people here were good folks. She wanted her daughters to grow up the same way she had, enjoying simple pleasures.

"Maybe a small hotel would be all right," she conceded. "And a small, very exclusive spa."

Sylvia grinned. "Let's wash off that masque.

You'll find you're a new woman. Then let's tackle the hair. I'm thinking a body wave will put the bounce back in your mane.''

AFTER FOUR DAYS in his new house, Eli was still living out of boxes. He supposed part of him didn't want to believe this move was permanent. But another part of him wondered how his split with Gwen could be anything but. She'd accused him of stealing from him. Granted, the evidence was compelling, but she hadn't even looked for another explanation.

But Eli was looking. A clever forger had deliberately set him up to take a fall, and he was going to figure out who that person was if it was the last thing he ever did. Then he was going to wave the proof in Gwen's face.

He sat at his dining room table with a pen and notebook, making a list of suspects. There weren't many.

Most obvious were the other tenants in Tanner's Boardinghouse. None of them had particularly welcomed Eli's arrival, especially at first. They all liked being Gwen's surrogate parents, and they were protective of her. A certain amount of resentment toward the man who'd gotten her pregnant and supposedly abandoned her was only natural. And the changes that had taken place in their comfortable routines could have fomented a quiet rage in one of them. Getting rid of Eli meant things could return to normal.

But he had a hard time believing any of the three—Stella, Irene or Oggie—could be responsible for framing him. Stella was so sweet. She just wanted everyone to be happy, and he couldn't imagine her doing anything so blatantly hateful. Irene was a little quieter, hiding behind her books, and who knew what was going on behind those thoughtful, intelligent eyes? And Oggie had often been openly hostile toward Eli.

Still, Oggie Lewis, school vice principal, a forger?

Another suspect was Bobby Larson. Bobby had been riding Eli since the moment he'd set foot in Jester. He made it no secret he wanted the property Eli had bought, so he could build his hotel. So Bobby had plenty of motive for getting rid of Eli. But breaking up his and Gwen's marriage made it much less likely Eli would sell the house he was renovating, now that he actually needed to live here. And he couldn't figure out how Bobby would have had access to Gwen's keys and Gwen's office. Although he dropped by sometimes, he never stayed for long, and he wouldn't normally be left alone in the house.

Others had easier access. What about Sylvia Rutledge? She was Gwen's best friend. Sylvia was known to always be in some sort of man trouble. She had a dim view of the whole male species. Maybe she resented Gwen's marriage—maybe she was jealous.

Reluctantly, Eli added Sylvia to the list.

He tried to think of others he'd seen coming and going in the house. There was Stella's friend, Wyla. Wyla wasn't the most pleasant person in the world, but Eli didn't see that she had any particular ax to grind with him. Oggie occasionally tutored students, and it was feasible one of them could dart into Gwen's open office and steal checks. But the forgery seemed more sophisticated than what a student could do—calculated, rather than a crime of opportunity.

Only one other person had held any resentment toward Eli, and that was Bud Farrell, the man with the wrecked Nash Coupe. He was certainly devious— he'd deliberately lied about the car insurance, and he'd stopped payment on his check though Eli had fulfilled his end of the bargain. He also had access to Eli's signature, on their contract. It was possible Gwen had left him alone in the house long enough that he could steal checks from her office.

He added Bud's name to the list. He intended to take his suspicions to Luke McNeil. The sheriff, who'd lived in Jester all his life, might have further insight into the personalities of the various suspects. He also probably had access to fraud and forgery experts at the state crime lab. Eli had kept the copies of the forged checks. The originals could be dusted for fingerprints.

The doorbell interrupted his prognostications. For the briefest of seconds his hopes rose as he imagined it was Gwen on his front porch, ready to apologize for doubting him, ready to help him find the real culprit. But of course it was just the FedEx man.

Eli signed for several packages. One contained a new microwave, which he'd ordered from a catalogue. That would come in handy. His kitchen was severely lacking in appliances, and he was getting tired of taking all his meals at The Brimming Cup. Not that the food wasn't great, but he was weary of the stares. Everyone in town knew he and Gwen had split up, though apparently no one knew why. At least Gwen hadn't spread it all over town that he was a thief.

Another of the packages contained a carburetor he'd been waiting for to repair a wonderful 1931 DeSoto SA6 Silver Dome. Jennifer McNeil, Luke's wife, had found it in the garage on the farm she'd inherited from her grandfather, Henry Faulkner. She recalled that he used to tinker with it when she visited Jester as a little girl, and she wanted it restored as a remembrance of him.

Glad for something to do other than take down old wallpaper, Eli took the part and headed for his garage to install it and see if he could get the car started.

Forty minutes later, the engine sputtered to life. Coughing from the copious exhaust pouring from the tail pipe, Eli gave the car a pat. ''See, old girl, I knew you could do it. Let's go for a spin, see if we can't blow some of that gunk out of your pipes.''

The engine coughed and sputtered and backfired, but it did move the car forward. Eli guided it slowly out of the garage and onto Main Street. He wouldn't go farther than he could walk, since the car could conk out on him at any time and the tires were so old they crunched. But he needed to get a feel for how the gears shifted.

As he drove past the boardinghouse, he looked up at Gwen's window and sighed. Hell, couldn't he go five minutes without thinking about her, without regretting the relationship they would never have?

They were bound inextricably because of the twins. He would probably know her the rest of his life, see her on a regular basis. How could he stop wanting her under those circumstances? How would he handle it if she fell in love with someone else and remarried?

The thought made him sick to his stomach.

GWEN DECIDED she did not like getting a permanent, and she didn't feel pampered at all. Rolling her thick hair up on rods had taken forever. Now she had her head in the sink, and Sylvia was pouring some noxious, cold, gluey stuff over each rod.

"Are you sure about this?" Gwen asked for the third time. "I don't want to end up looking like Shirley Temple."

"I used the biggest rods," Sylvia assured her, also for the third time. "You should end up with gentle waves, just like it was before you were pregnant."

"I'm going to be very upset if you're wrong."

"Trust me. Now, we'll just let that sit for a few minutes." She set a digital timer, a purple one to match the rest of the shop, then settled in the chair at the station next to Gwen's to go through a pile of mail.

"My gosh, what's all that?" Gwen asked, noting the huge stack the postman had delivered a few minutes ago.

"I subscribe to every magazine on earth," Sylvia admitted. "The phone solicitors started in the day I received the lottery check and haven't stopped since. I just can't tell them no."

"Always a problem for you," Gwen quipped.

Sylvia ignored the jab—probably because it was true. Sylvia adored men, she just didn't like them very much.

"Okay, we got *Glamour, Cosmopolitan, Today's Hairstyles,* and *Rolling Stone.*"

"*Rolling Stone*?"

"It's hip. I have to stay on top of the trends. Oh, here's the *Plain Talker.* Shall we see what our friend Harvey Brinkman has dug up about us today?"

"What's this 'we'? As I recall, your name has hardly been mentioned."

"That's because I live such a boring and unremarkable life." Sylvia opened the paper and thumbed through it. "Well, you'll be happy to know nothing made the front page. Wait, here's something on page three. Ah, very nice picture of Eli. Funny, he doesn't *look* like a rat."

"Eli? What's it say?" Gwen demanded. She started to sit up, but when the cold liquid tried to dribble down her neck, she relaxed.

"This appears to be an exposé on your husband." Sylvia scanned the article, frowning. "Did you know Eli is a consultant to the Smithsonian Institution?"

"What? Oh, Lord, where does Harvey come up with this stuff?"

"It says here Eli actually renovated some of the airplanes on display at the Air and Space Museum."

"He's never mentioned that to me. But then, he's

never told me *anything* about himself. His past is just this big, black hole. What else?''

''Oh. Oh, my.''

''Would you just read it?''

''He recently sold a two-million-dollar house in Denver. It was built into the side of a mountain, and it was powered with solar, thermal and wind energy. He built it himself.''

''Did you say two million—''

''Aw, Gwen, he was an orphan. Abandoned, left in a…oh, my God.''

''What?''

''He was left in a Dumpster. Had some health problems, never adopted, raised in foster care—''

Gwen put her hands over her ears. ''Stop! I can't stand this!''

''You mean he never told you any of this?''

''Not a word.''

''Well, no wonder he has money issues, if he had such a disadvantaged childhood.'' Sylvia rattled the paper as she continued reading. ''Um, Gwen, I think there's a problem.''

''What do you mean?''

''Your husband is worth over three million dollars.''

''He's—*what?*''

''Rich. Richer than you. Richer than you and me put together.'' Sylvia burst out laughing at the absurdity.

''But how could that be?'' Gwen cried in anguish. ''He's a mechanic!''

"He is, and I quote, the world's foremost expert on antique vehicle restoration."

"But why didn't he tell me he was rich?"

"The same reason he didn't tell you a lot of stuff. He doesn't like to talk about himself. Anyway, he probably figured you knew. But, Gwen, ask yourself this. Would a man worth three million dollars steal a few thousand dollars from you?"

"But...but his signature was on those checks."

"Do you think he'd be that stupid? If he didn't want to get caught, he would at least sign a fake name you wouldn't immediately recognize."

Eli might be a lot of things, but stupid wasn't one of them. Earlier, Gwen had reasoned that Eli had wanted to get caught, that his check-stealing stunt had been some sort of cry for help. Now, with blazing clarity, Gwen realized he hadn't signed those checks at all. Someone had framed him.

She sat up. "Eli's not stupid, but I am. How could I have possibly believed he would steal from me? I was so ready to believe the worst about him, and now I've driven him away with my accusations."

"It wasn't all your fault," Sylvia soothed. "He wasn't very open with you."

"He probably has very good reasons for keeping his past private. I hadn't earned his trust yet, that's all it was. I've made a terrible mistake." She stood and ripped off the purple plastic apron she'd been wearing to protect her clothes. "I've got to find him and apologize, before it's too late."

"Wait, Gwen," Sylvia called as Gwen headed for

the door. "Let me rinse the solution out of your hair."

"No time!" Gwen yelled over her shoulder as she hit the door. She couldn't bear to wait one second longer than was necessary. She might have to spend months or years convincing Eli to forgive her, and she wanted to get started right away.

"You forgot your coat!"

Gwen didn't care. She ran down Main Street as fast as she could. Customers poured out of The Brimming Cup and the barbershop to watch the spectacle of a hugely pregnant woman trying to sprint, but she didn't care about that, either.

She had to find Eli.

She tried his house first, but her repeated beating on the door—his doorbell didn't work—produced no answer. Undaunted, she ran around the corner to the garage, thinking surely he would be there. He was always in one of those two places.

But his two garage bays were empty, the office locked up.

"Dammit!" she screamed. This was intolerable. Was she supposed to just sit and wait for him? Where could he be?

Now she wished she'd remembered her coat. Her wet head was freezing. She decided to get a blanket from inside the boardinghouse, then wait on Eli's porch for his return.

After stepping inside her home, she paused for a few moments to savor the warmth and catch her breath. She was pathetically out of shape! She had a stitch in her side from running, and no amount of gasping for breath would cure it.

She should have done more walking, like her doctor had ordered. Well, no help for it now.

The babies apparently weren't very happy with her sudden exertion. It felt like they were having a prenatal martial arts tournament inside her belly.

"Take it easy, girls," she said as her breath finally normalized. "I won't run anymore, promise."

The house was quiet. Oggie was at school, and Irene was probably at the mystery book club she'd started at Ex Libris. Stella was probably here, though, because the front door was unlocked.

Unconcerned, Gwen walked through the entry hall into the living room, where one of Stella's afghans was draped over the camelback sofa. Gwen grabbed it and wrapped it around herself. Perfect.

She spun on her heel, intent on returning to Eli's, when something struck her as not quite right. She paused, thinking what it could be.

It was her office door. She'd carefully locked it after her argument with Eli, and she hadn't been in there since. But the door had been open when she'd passed.

She went to investigate. The door was in fact open, the lights off. She stepped inside and flipped on the light. Everything appeared undisturbed. Then she heard a rustling sound behind her. She whirled around and found Wyla Thorne standing behind the door, looking decidedly guilty.

"Wyla! What on earth are you—" Then Gwen saw what was in Wyla's hand. A wad of checks. *"You! You're the one who stole from me?"*

## Chapter Thirteen

There wasn't much point in Wyla denying she was guilty, since she'd been caught red-handed. So she went on the offensive. "That money should have been mine! It's only fair. I played the lottery every single week for three years!"

"Life's tough all over!" Gwen shot back. "What you did may have cost me my marriage."

"It must not have been much of a marriage, then." Wyla's slight smile only infuriated Gwen further—probably because Gwen feared there was a grain of truth in the ugly quip. She snatched the blank checks out of Wyla's hand and tossed them onto her desk.

"I don't understand, Wyla. You didn't even need the money. Your farm was just about the only solvent one in the county!"

"I was comfortable, but I didn't drive a Mercedes. I only wanted the same things all you other girls had—clothes, jewelry." She firmed her mouth. "A man."

Gwen refused to soften at the glisten of tears in

Wyla's eyes. "You've had two husbands. You couldn't let me have just one?"

Stella appeared in the doorway, looking stricken. "What on earth is going on here?"

"Wyla's been stealing from me," Gwen said, never taking her eyes off Wyla. "She stole checks from my checkbook and forged Eli's name on them."

Stella shook her head in denial. "You must be mistaken, Gwen. Wyla would never do a thing like that." She looked at her friend. "It's a mistake, right?"

Wyla said nothing.

"I'm calling the sheriff," Gwen said, reaching for the phone.

Suddenly Wyla made a break for it. She pushed Stella out of the way and dashed for the front door. Gwen had never seen Wyla move quite that fast before.

Gwen set down the phone. She would deal with Wyla later. Right now, she had a marriage to save.

"Oh, Gwen, I'm so sorry," Stella said tearfully.

"What? Why? It's not your fault."

"I'm the one who let her into this house and befriended her. I left her alone. I knew Wyla was bitter about not playing the lottery the week it hit, but I had no idea she would do anything criminal."

Gwen gave Stella a hug. "It's not your fault, and I don't want to hear any more about it. Eli told me I was far too lax with security, even for a small town. I left my keys lying around, half the time I didn't lock the office. It's a wonder someone didn't rip me off before now. But it's over and done. Later I'll go to the sheriff's office and file a complaint. But right now, I have to find Eli.''

''He's out test-driving Jennifer McNeil's DeSoto. I saw him leave a few minutes ago. I'm sure he'll be back soon.''

''I'm going to wait for him outside, then.''

''Oh, honey, it's cold out there. And your hair—is that a permanent wave?''

Gwen put a hand to her head. ''I was in such a hurry I didn't even let Sylvia rinse me off.''

Stella gasped. ''Had she put the neutralizer on yet?''

''The stinky stuff?''

''No, the nicer-smelling stuff that stops the curling action.''

''I don't think so.''

''Jiminy Christmas, you're going to look like Richard Simmons. Come with me.'' Stella grabbed Gwen by the arm and dragged her into the kitchen. Moments later she had Gwen's head in the sink and was rinsing out the gooey stuff. ''You better go back to The Crowning Glory and finish the job, or you might end up bald.''

Gwen was sure Stella was exaggerating. ''I don't have time for that. Just—ow! What the hell's going on?'' Gwen leaned against the counter, gasping for breath as the sharp pain peaked, then subsided.

Stella put a hand to her mouth. ''Oh, honey, you're not going into labor, are you?''

Gwen shook her head in denial. ''Absolutely not. I instructed the twins not to make an appearance until

their due date. It was probably just something I ate.''
She grabbed a dishcloth and patted her head as dry
as she could get it. That was when her water broke.

''You better sit down, honey,'' Stella said. ''Do
you want me to call Doc Perkins?''

''No. I'll just wait until Eli gets back, and he can
drive me to the hospital. There's no reason to panic,
right?''

''Babies take hours and hours to be born,'' Stella
said reassuringly.

''I'll just sit by the front window.''

Stella helped Gwen to the front parlor, where she
sat on the sofa with a good view of Main Street. Then
she picked up the phone that sat on the end table and
called the sheriff.

''I was just curious if you'd seen Eli,'' she asked,
sounding much calmer than she felt. ''I really need
to talk to him.''

''No, I haven't, Gwen,'' Luke said. ''But I'll keep
an eye out for him.''

''Thanks.'' She hung up, wondering if she should
just let Stella drive her to Pine Run. But she simply
couldn't envision having the babies without Eli right
there for the whole thing. She was counting on the
shared experience to bring them back together. If
nothing else, at least Eli would have to feel sorry for
her, having to go through labor.

THE CAR OVERHEATED just beyond the city limits
sign, steam pouring out from under the hood. That bit
of luck was just about par for the course, given Eli's

black mood. He turned off the ignition and climbed out, glad he'd brought his toolbox along. He didn't relish the thought of getting someone to tow the car back to the garage.

It was cold today, and tiny, dry flakes of snow drifted out of the sky in occasional flurries. Eli wondered if it was snowing yet at Silver Creek, his favorite little ski resort. He thought briefly of packing up and heading home, taking a vacation, forgetting everything.

But then he realized that Jester *was* home. The quirky little town and its people had grown on him. He'd missed his communal breakfasts with Stella and Irene and Oggie, trying to choke down Stella's muffins without grimacing, enduring Oggie's censorious stares and Stella's clumsy matchmaking attempts. If he left here, he would miss his daily dose of soup at The Brimming Cup, listening to the gossip. He would miss reading the *Plain Talker,* so full of folksy news and bad grammar and yellow journalism courtesy of Harvey Brinkman. He would miss the silly seasonal decorations that adorned the streetlights on Main Street.

Ah, hell, who was he kidding? He could no more leave Jester than he could stop breathing. His children were here. His wife was here. Despite Gwen's lack of faith in him, he loved her. He wouldn't divorce her. He wouldn't marry someone else. He would stay here and hash this thing out.

And that, he realized, was something he'd never done before. He tended to walk away from problems, to simply move on when things got complicated. Maybe it had something to do with his foster home experiences. Whenever things got uncomfortable, when he got to be too hard to handle, he would simply be moved to a new family. No permanent bonds had ever been established, so moving on was no problem.

But he couldn't do that now. For better or worse, Gwen and those two children she carried were his family now. Shelly and Dan at the diner were his family. He wasn't exactly sure what to do with one now that he had it, but he was determined to figure that out.

After giving the overheated radiator a chance to cool, Eli opened the DeSoto's creaky hood and looked inside. After a little tinkering, he saw the problem. The radiator hose had a big hole in it. Lucky he'd brought some electrical tape with him. The emergency repair would perhaps get him back to the garage. He went to work, though his progress was hampered by his cold hands.

As he worked, he was aware of a car approaching, then slowing, then stopping. He looked up to see Paula Pratt's eggplant P.T. Cruiser pulling up beside him. Paula's passenger was the mayor.

Oh, terrific. Just what he needed—another argument with that officious twerp.

Bobby Larson climbed out of the car. "You stay in the car where it's warm, hon—Paula. I'll just be a minute." He slammed the door and walked over to where Eli worked. Eli tried his best to ignore the mayor.

"Morning, Eli. Nice car you got there. Do you need some help? I could call Tex's Garage on my radio and have a tow truck here in no time."

"I've got it under control," Eli said, then added a grudging, "Thanks for the offer."

"Listen, Eli. Seems you and I got off on the wrong foot. I believe I owe you an apology."

Eli looked up, suspicious. What had prompted this sudden change of heart?

"Apology accepted," he said blandly. If he was going to live here the rest of his life, he might as well try to get along with the mayor.

"When you moved here and took up with Gwen, I assumed you were an opportunist, her being a new millionaire and all. You can't blame me for wanting to protect Gwen. She's like a daughter to me, you know."

"Yes, you've mentioned that."

"But after I read the paper today, I realized I must've been wrong about you. You're quite successful in your own right. You obviously don't need Gwen's money."

"The paper?"

"You haven't seen it?"

"No, 'fraid not." Eli returned to his repairs, wishing the mayor would go away.

"Harvey Brinkman," Bobby said. "Nice article, for a change."

"I'll be sure to read it." He'd put the hose back on, then realized he would need some water for the radiator. "Damn."

"So that brings Jester's millionaire ranks up to thirteen—do you need help with something?"

"You don't happen to have a jug of antifreeze in your car, do you?"

"No, but Paula has a bottle of spring water."

"That would do," Eli said hopefully.

Bobby signaled for Paula to roll down her window. After a brief argument, Paula surrendered her half-liter bottle of water, still almost full. With murmured thanks, Eli dumped it into the radiator and screwed the cap back on.

"You know," Bobby said, continuing the conversation as if there'd been no interruption, "the other Main Street Millionaires have contributed quite a lot to civic improvements. They had the statue in front of the town hall of Caroline Peterson and her horse Jester cleaned up. Shelly fixed up the church and Jack Hartman bought some new playground equipment for the school children."

Ah, now things were becoming clear. Bobby was being nice because he wanted Eli's money. "What is it you'd like me to contribute to?" Eli asked point-blank. Bobby was pretty transparent.

He smiled unctuously. "Glad you asked. Jester only needs one thing to make it a real, first-class town, and that's a hotel."

Eli should have known. "I seem to remember the project was a no-go because a suitable site couldn't be secured."

"And that's where you come in," Bobby said quickly. "You and Gwen are sitting on some prime real estate. The two lots together, plus Mac's Auto Repair, would be a perfect site.''

Before Eli could even take a deep breath to tell Bobby he was barking up the wrong tree, Bobby continued. ''Now, wait, hear me out. You and Gwen, with millions between you, you don't need to be running a boardinghouse. Do you really want your wife to continue as a domestic laborer? That doesn't reflect very well on you.''

He would never in a million years want to drag Gwen away from her boardinghouse. On those occasions when she felt well enough to cook and bake, Eli had seen that she was in her element. She was a nurturer by nature. Even with two babies to care for, she would never want to give up the business her grandmother—or was it her great-grandmother?—had started. It was her legacy.

But Eli was curious about how far Bobby would go.

''I do wish Gwen would slow down,'' Eli said. ''That boardinghouse is an albatross around our necks. We can't travel, and we'll end up spending our leisure time on repairs and upkeep.''

''Then ask Gwen to reconsider my offer. Two hundred grand is more than she could get on the open market. I'll build the hotel with or without her cooperation, you know. One place or another. And once the hotel is in place, no one will want to stay at an old-fashioned boardinghouse. She ought to get while the gettin's good.''

Eli barely resisted popping Bobby's fat face,

though he didn't want to add to his reputation for brawling. Did the mayor really think he was making friends with Eli by threatening his wife?

Paula Pratt rolled down the window. "Come on, Robert, it's cold. I want to get back."

"You go on without me, Paula," Bobby said. "I'm helping Eli with his car."

With a petulant frown, Paula rolled up her window and sped away.

"Where will you build if you don't get Gwen's and my property?" Eli asked as he wiped his hands with a rag.

"The Town Park. Now that the pavilion is gone, there's nothing to stop me from acquiring the land."

"Yeah, pretty convenient, the pavilion collapsing like that." Eli gave a little chuckle.

Bobby laughed, too. "Yeah, convenient. That's one way to put it. The thing was rotted through—it was going to fall down anyway, and it could have happened when it was full of people. The way I see it, we were real lucky only one person was injured, and that wasn't too serious."

"So I guess you did the town a favor."

"Saved the city a bucket of money, too. Because it was an accident, insurance paid to have it cleaned up. If it hadn't collapsed, we'd have had to pay someone to tear it down."

A chill worked its way up Eli's spine. He'd just been on a fishing expedition. He'd never in a million years expected Bobby Larson to admit he'd committed a criminal act. Now, what was he going to do about it? Would Eli's word be enough so that Luke McNeil could arrest Bobby? Luke had said the state crime lab found fingerprints on the support beam, where the saboteur had steadied himself on a ladder while loosening the bolts that held the roof together. Maybe Eli could at least convince Luke to take Bobby's fingerprints and make a comparison.

"So," Eli said conversationally as he closed the hood, "how do you stand for investors? If Gwen thought we could get a good return, maybe she would consider selling the houses and investing the proceeds in the hotel."

"I've got all the projections back at my office," Bobby said excitedly. "There might be room for one more investor, especially if you could help me acquire the property I need."

"And if I can't?"

"Well, investors are always welcome. We can go take a look at the park property, if you want. I can walk you through the floor plan."

"Let's see if we can get this baby started." Eli climbed behind the wheel and turned the key. The engine purred to life, with only a couple of coughs this time.

Bobby wedged his portly body into the passenger seat. "People must've been smaller back when these cars were built."

With his heart thumping, Eli turned the car around and drove back into town. He casually wheeled it into a parking spot in front of the sheriff's office.

"Why are you parking here?" Bobby asked.

"I promised the sheriff I'd pick up some, um, papers." That was the best lie Eli could come up with in a pinch. "Be right back." He jumped out of the car and sprinted into the sheriff's office, praying Luke would be there.

He was, sitting behind his desk filling out some kind of form. He looked up when Eli entered. "Eli. Funny you should drop by. Gwen called here, trying to find you."

Eli's heart all but stopped. "Is she in labor?"

"I'm ashamed to say I didn't even think of that. But she sounded fine. She just wants to talk to you."

A rush of unexpected pleasure filled Eli's body. His wife wanted to talk. That was promising. Unfortunately, she would have to wait just a few minutes longer.

"Luke, I don't have much time to explain this to you. I want you to arrest Bobby Larson."

*"What?"*

"He just admitted to me he's the one who sabotaged the pavilion. He did it to clear the way for his hotel—and to defraud the insurance company, apparently. He was going to show me the proposed hotel site at the park—I led him to believe I might want to invest."

"Hell, I thought all along he was the most likely suspect."

"Then you believe me?"

"Of course I believe you. Why wouldn't I?"

"Because you've known the mayor all your life, and I haven't lived here long enough to earn anyone's trust.'' He was beginning to understand how that worked, now. Trust wasn't an automatic right. It had to be earned, and that took time.

Luke shrugged. ''I don't see why you'd lie about a thing like that. Let's go have a talk with His Honor.'' Luke stood and shrugged into a leather jacket, then both men stepped outside.

Luke opened the passenger door of the DeSoto. ''Bobby. Sorry to leave you out in the cold like this, but Eli's and my business is taking a bit longer than expected. Would you step inside the office, please?''

Bobby darted a nervous gaze to Eli, then back to Luke. Then he climbed out of the car. ''I think maybe I'll just walk back to the town hall. I can show Eli…what I wanted to show him…some other time.''

''You mean, show him the place where the pavilion used to stand? The pavilion you tampered with in order to make it collapse? The pavilion that could have killed Melinda Hartman?''

Bobby looked frightened. ''Now, no one was supposed to be in that pavilion. You can't pin Melinda's concussion on me.''

''It was just supposed to collapse,'' Luke said, ''so that your hotel plan would look more attractive to the town council, is that it?''

Bobby shot an accusing look at Eli. ''What did you say to him?''

Eli shrugged. ''Just told Luke what you told me.'' He turned to Luke. ''Bobby did say he never meant for anyone to be hurt.''

''That's right,'' Bobby said hastily. ''And tell him

the rest. I did it because the thing was going to collapse on its own anyway. It was full of termites! If I hadn't hastened the pavilion's demise, it might have fallen down on fifty or a hundred people!''

Luke looked at Eli. ''Well, that was easier than I expected it to be. Bobby, come along with me. You're under arrest for reckless disregard, criminal mischief, public endangerment, insurance fraud and anything else I can come up with.''

''You can't arrest me!'' Bobby blustered. ''I'm the mayor!''

''Mayors are not immune to arrest,'' Luke said, blocking Bobby's way when it looked like the mayor would try to just walk away. ''They're not above the law, either.''

Bobby drew himself up. ''I'll have your job, Luke McNeil.''

''I think it's the other way around,'' Luke said as he pulled handcuffs from a leather case. ''Now, are you going to step inside, or do we do this the hard way?''

Bobby slapped Luke's hand away as the sheriff tried to escort him toward the office. In a movement fast as a striking snake, Luke had Bobby against the car, his hands cuffed behind his back, while Bobby blustered and cursed.

Eli thought this was just about the wildest thing he'd seen since arriving in Jester. But that was before he saw his wife barreling toward him down the sidewalk, her hair in curlers and an afghan around her shoulders.

"Eli, oh, Eli, I'm so glad I spotted that DeSoto." She skidded to a stop, huffing and puffing. "I've made a terrible mistake. I was so dumb to think you could have stolen anything from me. It was Wyla Thorne all along."

"What?" all three men said at the same time. Even Bobby had stopped struggling and cursing to find out more about the latest scandal.

"Wyla stole checks from me and…forged your…" She didn't finish the sentence as a look of agony came over her face and she clutched her abdomen. Eli darted toward her and caught her as she was about to collapse on the sidewalk.

"Gwen," Luke said, "are you okay?"

She opened her eyes. "I'm fine. Just a little labor."

No words had ever struck Eli with such mortal fear. "Someone call an ambulance!"

Luke shook his head. "It takes forever for an ambulance to get here from Pine Run. Better just take her over to the clinic and let Doc Perkins or Conner O'Rourke——"

"No," Gwen objected. "I know both doctors are excellent, but if the babies are born now, they'll be premature. They'll need the neonatal unit in Pine Run. Luke, can you drive us?" She looked at Luke, then Bobby, then Luke again. "Why is the mayor in handcuffs?"

"Long story," Luke said. "But I am a little tied up." He pulled his keys from his pocket and tossed them to Eli. "Take my truck. Run the siren if you have to."

Eli felt a little weak-kneed himself as he helped Gwen to Luke's SUV. He was amazed Luke would trust him with an official vehicle. He was sure the sheriff was breaking all kinds of laws.

Just as he was about to close the passenger door, Sylvia Rutledge appeared to give Gwen her coat. "You are going to catch pneumonia," she scolded. "You're completely crazy. You know that, right?"

"Yes," Gwen readily agreed.

"Call and let me know what's happening, okay?"

Gwen nodded. She looked scared, but not half as scared as Eli felt. He ran around to the driver's side, climbed behind the wheel, and peeled off.

"How long have you been having contractions?" he demanded.

"I'm not sure. I've felt peculiar all day, like the babies were doing karate moves in there. Still, Eli, really, there's no point in speeding. Babies take hours to be—owwww!"

Eli resisted the urge to stamp down on the accelerator. He was already going above the speed limit, and there was always the chance of hitting a patch of ice. Visualizing the consequences of winding up in a ditch, he forced himself to slow down to a reasonable speed. He took several deep breaths.

"Maybe you should let me drive," Gwen suggested with a shaky laugh.

"I'm fine. You just tell those girls not to be so impatient."

"Um, Eli? I don't think…they're listening."

He looked at her and realized she was contracting

again. "This is ridiculous. No one goes into labor and has a baby five minutes later."

"Tell that to Thing One and Thing Two!"

"But your water hasn't broken yet."

"Oh, yes, it did. A while ago."

"Gwen, what were you waiting for?"

"For you!" Her eyes filled with tears. "I was not going through this without you. Now pull over."

"What?"

"*Pull over!* You can't drive and deliver babies at the same time."

## Chapter Fourteen

Eli's eyes were filled with raw panic, but Gwen felt oddly calm. She'd been waiting for this moment for so long. Now, when it was here, it felt a lot different than she'd expected. She'd thought she would be frightened out of her wits. But some latent maternal instinct had taken over. She would be fine, and her babies would be fine. With Eli here, nothing could go wrong.

"See if you can figure out Luke's radio and call for an ambulance," Gwen said serenely. "I'm moving to the back seat where I can stretch out."

"Are you serious? You're actually going to have the babies *now?*"

"I don't know." She stopped as another contraction hit, this one harder than the others. She panted through the pain. Okay, it wasn't so bad. She could do this. "But I ought to be prepared, just in case." She opened the door, climbed out, and somehow managed to get herself into the back seat without major difficulty. She dragged Stella's afghan with her. It had become her security blanket.

Eli blathered something into the radio. Through blind luck he'd managed to reach the sheriff's office in Pine Run. After some convoluted explanations, the dispatch officer agreed to send an ambulance.

Eli looked through the grillwork that separated front seat from back. "How are you doing?"

Gwen had already removed the necessary clothing. She'd spread her coat under her, to protect Luke's car, and she'd spread the afghan over her legs for warmth.

"I'm doing fine. You want to join me?"

"Me? Back there?"

"Someone has to catch the babies."

He went pale. "Gwen, I can't deliver babies."

But her next contraction overrode his objection. "Eliiiii! Don't wimp out on me now."

He scrambled from the front to the back seat. "Tell me what to do."

"There's a first-aid kit under the front seat," she said. "See if you can find anything useful."

"Like what?" He pulled the box out. "Bingo. Sterile rubber gloves. And a moist towelette. And cotton swabs."

"And I'm sure—" She stopped to pant.

Eli squeezed her hand. "It's okay, baby. You're doing great."

"...there might be a blanket in the back. It might not be sterile, but it would help keep the babies warm."

Sure enough, Eli found a blanket in the cargo area.

"Eli? Something's happening."

"I'm right here, sweetheart. Just take your time."

"I'm so sorry, Eli," Gwen blurted out. "I never should have doubted you. It was Wyla. She was mad about not buying a lottery ticket the week we won. She forged your signature—"

"Don't worry about that now."

"I have to. I refuse to let my babies be born while we're still fighting."

"We're not fighting anymore."

"Then just let me talk. It keeps my mind off the pain. Is there any chance you'll ever forgive me?"

"Oh, baby, I do forgive you. Anyway, it was half my fault. You were right to be suspicious of me. The evidence was piling up, and I wasn't lifting a finger to calm your doubts. I just expected you to totally trust me. I think in some twisted way—breathe, Gwen."

She started panting, like they'd taught her in childbirth class. "Go…on."

"I had some crazy idea that real love meant automatic trust."

"But I should have trusted you," she said.

"No, Gwen. Not when I wasn't being open with you. That's the flip side of trust. I wasn't willing to trust you with things from my past, especially the less pleasant things."

"Like the bankruptcy."

"I paid back every one of my creditors. It took a few years, but I did. If I'd just told you that, it would have put you somewhat at ease."

"Yes, it would have," she agreed.

"Oh, and the fact I changed my name? There's no

dark secret behind that. When I was sixteen, and I wanted to get my driver's license—uh, Gwen, something definitely is happening.''

"Okay, don't panic, just keep talking. When you…got your…driver's license…''

"I had to have a birth certificate. That's when I found out my real name. Oh, my God, there's a head. I think you're supposed to push.''

"I'm pushing. Just keep talking. What was your real name?''

"John Doe Number Three.''

Gwen wanted to cry. How horrible! But she was too excited and too happy to burst into tears. She was about to become a mother.

"Eli Garrett is a very nice name.'' She paused and scrunched up her face.

"Breathe.''

"I'm breathing. Did you pick out your name yourself?''

"No. I was always called that. Some nice nurse or social worker picked it out. They just neglected to put it on—oh! Oh, jeez, oh, jeez, this is scary.''

She gave one final push.

"It's a girl,'' Eli said needlessly, his voice thick with emotion. "Will you look at that?''

Gwen laughed and cried at the same time. The infant was unbelievably tiny, but she looked perfect. Then Gwen realized the baby wasn't crying. "Eli? She's too quiet.''

Eli held the baby upside down. "C'mon, little one, get some air into those lungs.''

Obediently the baby coughed, then started up a thready cry. His hands shaking, Eli handed the baby to Gwen, who wrapped it in the blanket. She barely had time to catch her breath before the second baby made an appearance. It all happened so quickly, Gwen didn't even have a chance to appreciate the first one before she had two in her arms.

A siren in the distance was the most reassuring noise Gwen had ever heard.

"Look what you did," Eli said in awe as he gazed on his daughters.

"No, what *we* did. It's not like I could have conceived them by myself. How do you feel about Bonnie and Belinda?"

"Just like that?"

"I think I had to see them first. Anyway, after what you just told me, I want to be sure they have names before the birth certificates end up with Thing One and Thing Two on them."

He grinned. "Bonnie and Belinda suit me fine." He paused. "Gwen?"

"Yes, Eli?"

"I love you. I've loved you all along, but I didn't want to admit it, even to myself. I was too afraid you didn't love me back. I guess that's why I was trying to make you prove it."

Gwen's eyes, already teary, overflowed. "Oh, Eli, silly man. I fell in love with you that morning when I woke up with those ridiculous teddy bears on my bed. I knew a man who could walk through an airport carrying those bears for his daughters was one who was worth keeping. Do you want to hold them?''

Eli's face once again reflected panic. He backed into the farthest corner of the back seat. "No, no, they look perfectly happy where they are.''

"Eli Garrett, are you afraid of these teeny, tiny babies?''

"A little. Are they breathing?''

"Yes, they're breathing. They're perfect. And we're going to be fine—aren't we?''

"We're going to be fantastic.''

Gwen closed her eyes and took a deep breath of satisfaction. In the coming hours, as doctors poked and prodded and applauded her performance and complimented her beautiful babies, she could do nothing but offer a dazed smile. Her life had been transformed from pure misery to bliss in the span of a few short hours.

Maybe she and Eli would have found their way back together eventually, but she would forever believe it was the birth of their twins that had hastened the reconciliation. Bonnie and Belinda really were Fortune's Twins, but not for the reasons Harvey Brinkman believed. Her good fortune had nothing to do with winning the lottery, and everything to do with her new and wonderful family.

"LET'S CALL this meeting to order," said Dev Devlin. No one was really in charge of the Jester Merchant's Association, but since Dev was hosting the meeting at The Heartbreaker Saloon, he acted as master of ceremonies.

Present at the meeting were Dev, Amanda, and the youngest of their four adopted children, two-year-old Betsy, curled in her mother's lap; Dean Kenning and Finn Hollis, who had set up a game of dominoes in case the meeting got boring; Sam and Ruby Cade; Sylvia Rutledge; Shelly and Conner O'Rourke, Shelly so pregnant Eli wondered if *she* was about to deliver twins; Jack and Melinda Hartman and their dog, Buck, who'd sneaked in on their heels; Luke and Jennifer McNeil; and Gwen and Eli along with Bonnie and Belinda. Eli had known it was folly bringing babies to the merchant's meeting, but after two weeks the twins were strong enough to venture out, and everyone wanted to hold them.

"Who's got old business to discuss?" Dev asked.

"I do," Dean said. "It's regarding the hotel."

A collective groan rose from the group.

"I just thought we ought to have a formal vote, so when I attend the town council meeting next week, I can report that the Merchants Association is unanimously against the project."

"With Bobby going to jail," Ruby pointed out, "it's not like the hotel was a happening thing, anyway."

"I know," Dean said. "But I just want to make things official. I'm calling for a vote. All in favor of the hotel, raise your hand."

Not one hand went up.

"All against?"

Everyone raised their hands. Just then, the door to the bar burst open, and a lovely blond-haired woman with a great tan burst into the room. All eyes were on her.

"What'd I miss?" she asked breathlessly. "I want to vote, too."

Ruby jumped out of her chair and rushed to hug the newcomer. "Honor Lassiter, you are in big trouble. You've been gone two months, and all I got were three lousy postcards!"

"Well, I was *busy*," she said with a grin as she pulled a chair up to the group of tables.

"We were just voting on the hotel project," Finn said.

"Against," Honor said.

So, this was the infamous Honor Lassiter. She was Ruby's partner in The Mercantile and one of the lottery winners. Eli had heard all about her from Finn and Dean. After dithering for months about what to do with her money, she'd suddenly packed up and left town to go on an around-the-world vacation. The circumstances had been a bit suspicious, according to Gwen. Honor wasn't the impulsive type.

Honor looked around the room, her eyes taking in everything—including Jester's newest residents. "Oh, my gosh, Gwen, are those both yours? And what the heck did you do to your hair?"

Gwen patted the cloud of tight auburn curls that cascaded around her shoulders. "Perm accident."

"Not my fault," Sylvia piped in, which she did any time anyone mentioned Gwen's new do.

Honor redirected her attention toward the twins. "Can I hold them?"

"Wait your turn," said Shelly, who was cuddling Bonnie while Conner, a pediatrician, held Belinda with practiced ease. "Besides, I need the experience."

Dev set a glass of white wine in front of Honor. "There. Now quit disrupting the meeting. When we're done, you can tell us all about your world travels."

"But don't you want to know why I'm against the hotel?" Honor asked.

"'Cause it's a dumb idea?" Jennifer ventured.

"No. Because I've decided what I'll do with my money. Well, some of it, anyway. I'm going to open a bed and breakfast." She looked at Gwen. "If it's okay with you, Gwen."

Gwen shrugged. "No complaints here. Eli has the perfect house for you, already fixed up—the old Carter place. I'd be more than happy for you to host Harvey Brinkman next time he comes to town."

"Did I hear my name taken in vain?"

A collective groan arose from the assemblage as the reporter in question sauntered into the room, a photographer trailing behind, trying to look invisible.

"Who let you out of the asylum, Harvey?" asked Conner, though there was no real bite in the comment. The residents of Jester had come to feel a reluctant affection for Harvey, despite his sensational stories. Harvey had developed a real interest in the town of Jester and the effects, good and bad, the lottery win had had on the town. His stories had gradually gained more substance and less flash and fluff.

"I really have to stay on you guys, now that my main snitch has left town." Harvey's "main snitch," as it turned out, was Wyla Thorne. Feeling vengeful after losing out on the lottery jackpot, she'd been feeding tidbits to Harvey for months—including the time and place of Gwen and Eli's wedding. After her forgery had come to light, she'd skipped town. Luke was optimistic about catching her, though. She'd left behind a very lucrative hog farm.

Eli still hadn't quite forgiven Harvey for the disgraceful display at the Pine Run courthouse, but Harvey, on threat of dismissal from the paper, had apologized in writing. He'd been a little better since then.

"So, what'd I miss?" Harvey asked, grabbing a chair as if he were one of the gang. He pulled up next to Honor. "Hey, doll, when did you blow back into town? Wanta give me a little exclusive when the meeting's over?" He waggled his eyebrows suggestively.

Honor grimaced. "In your dreams, Brinkman. Can we get back to business? Eli, I'd be delighted to talk to you about your house. It would be perfect."

Dev cleared his throat. "Any more old business? No? Okay, how about new business? I believe Shelly wanted to say something about the Thanksgiving streetlamp decorations."

"I was thinking neon turkeys."

Another groan.

"Just kidding. Really, what I wanted to do was turn

the responsibility over to someone else, since I'm going to be very busy." She patted her tummy. "I'll pay for the decorations."

"There's no reason you should pay for everything, Shelly," Ruby said. "You've already done a lot."

"But I haven't finished my list yet." Last winter, Shelly had put up a list of proposed town improvements at The Brimming Cup and asked her patrons to vote on which project to attack first. She'd since been working her way down the list.

"I think we should have a permanent list of improvements that we keep adding to," said Sam. "And all the merchants can donate a certain amount every month into a fund."

"We can put up suggestion boxes in different locations," said Melinda. "And we can let the townspeople continue to vote on what they'd like next. That way, the town will grow and improve, but slowly, at a pace that's comfortable for us."

"And no developers," said Gwen with a shudder. "No big hotels or shopping malls or tacky tourist attractions."

"And how about we change the street names back?" suggested Doc Perkins. "I'm tired of my office being on Lottery Lane and my house on Big Draw Drive. It's embarrassing."

"And I want to replace the duct-taped screen at Pop's," Gwen said.

"Aw, Gwen, that's my legacy," Dev complained. "The kids love pointing it out to their friends and bragging that their dad did that with a bottle rocket, back when he was a juvenile delinquent.''

"We need to modernize the medical clinic," said Shelly. "So we can handle real emergencies here in Jester.''

"And we've *got* to rebuild the pavilion," said Melinda.

"Put all these ideas in the suggestion box," said Conner. "Shall we vote? All in favor of funding city projects as voted on by the townspeople, from a fund created by the Merchants Association, raise your hand.''

The motion passed unanimously, of course.

"Shelly, I'll take over the streetlamp decorations," Jennifer offered.

"Great." Dev rubbed his hands together. "Any more new business? If not, there's a round on the house for everybody.''

"Wait a minute," said Finn. "There is one more thing. The town council is holding a special election for mayor, to replace Bobby. The only person who's expressed any interest in running is Paula Pratt.''

Another groan.

"I'll bet she was holding the ladder while Bobby unfastened the bolts on the pavilion," Jack Hartman grumbled.

"We've got to field a candidate. Anybody can beat Paula. They wouldn't even have to campaign. But we need a warm body.''

"Is there a residency requirement?" Eli asked.

Gwen looked at first surprised, then pleased. He

probably should have talked this over with her first, he realized. He'd come a long way in the sharing department, but he still sometimes had to be reminded.

"If there's a residency requirement, we'll overlook it," Dean said. "You thinking of tossing your hat into the ring, Eli?"

"I'd be honored. If you all want me. I mean, I'm still something of an outsider."

The applause and whistles were deafening.

"Of course we want you, Eli," said Amanda. "Fresh eyes are just what the town leadership needs. Otherwise, those old fossils on the town council—present company excluded, Dean—will just settle for what we've always had."

In less than ten minutes, someone had produced a petition and every registered voter in the room had signed it. Without even trying, Eli had a committee to collect the rest of the necessary signatures to get him on the ballot, a volunteer to make campaign signs and buttons, a speech writer and an image consultant.

"Not that you really need a new image," Sylvia added hastily. "You're pretty cute the way you are." She winked at Gwen.

The instant support of his fellow merchants surprised Eli, but he supposed it shouldn't have. That was just how Jester was. The people here *did* trust and accept him. All he'd had to do was open up a little himself, and they fell all over themselves to be his friends.

Gwen, his very best friend, leaned over and whispered, "Are you sure about this? If it's what you want, I'll support you a hundred percent."

"Yes, it's what I want. And thank you." He kissed her on the nose, then couldn't resist another, slightly more prolonged kiss on her mouth. "I can't think of a better way to give back to a town that's given me my first real home."

Gwen smiled and hooked her arm in his. "This town's lucky to have you. And so am I."

The warm feeling in his heart grew and expanded into every square inch of his being, until no part of him was left in darkness.

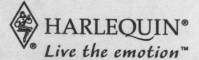

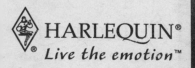

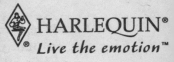

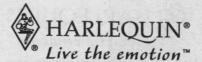

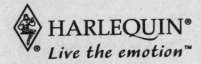